FAY
WELDON

Angel, All Innocence
and other stories

BLOOMSBURY
CLASSICS

'Alopecia', 'Man with no Eyes', 'Angel, All Innocence' and 'Weekend' are included in *Watching Me, Watching You* (Hodder and Stoughton, 1981); 'Horrors of the Road' and 'In the Great War' are included in *Polaris and Other Stories* (Hodder and Stoughton, 1985); 'Subject to Diary', 'Ind Aff'; or 'Out of Love in Sarajevo', 'Down the Clinical Disco', 'Un Crime Maternel' and 'The Day the World Came to Somerset' are included in *Moon over Minneapolis; or why she wouldn't stay* (HarperCollins, 1991). The publishers are grateful to Hodder Headline for permission to reprint stories from the first two collections and to Sheil Land Associates for the stories from the third.

This selection published 1995
© Fay Weldon 1981, 1985, 1991

This selection © Giles Gordon 1995
The moral right of the author has been asserted.
Bloomsbury Publishing Plc, 2 Soho Square,
London W1V 6HB
A CIP catalogue record for this book is available
from the British Library

ISBN 0 7475 21042

Typeset in Great Britain by
Hewer Text Composition Services, Edinburgh
Printed in Great Britain by St Edmundsbury Press
Jacket design by Jeff Fisher

CONTENTS

Man with no Eyes

Edgar, Minette, Minnie and Mona.

In the evenings three of them sit down to play Monopoly. Edgar, Minette and Minnie. Mona, being only five sleeps upstairs, alone, in the little back bedroom, where roses, growing up over the porch and along under the thatch, thrust dark companionable heads through the open lattice window. Edgar and Minnie, father and daughter, face each other across the table. Both, he in his prime, she in early adolescence, are already bronzed from the holiday sun, blue eyes bright and eager in lean faces, dull red hair bleached to brightness by the best summer the Kent coast has seen, they say, since 1951 – a merciful God allowing, it seems, the glimmer of His smile to shine again on poor humiliated England. Minette, Edgar's wife, sits at the kitchen end of the table. The ladderback chair nearest the porch remains empty. Edgar says it is uncomfortable. Minnie keeps the bank. Minette doles out the property cards.

Thus, every evening this holiday, they have arranged themselves around the table, and taken up their allotted tasks. They do it almost wordlessly, for Edgar does not care for babble. Who does? Besides, Mona might wake, think she was missing something, and insist on joining in.

How like a happy family we are, thinks Minette, pleased, shaking the dice. Minette's own face is pink and shiny from the sun and her nose is peeling. Edgar thinks hats on a beach are affected (an affront, as it were, to nature's generosity) so Minette is content to pay the annual penalty summer holidays impose on her fair complexion and fine mousy hair. Her mouth is swollen from the sun, and her red arms and legs are stiff and bumpy with midge bites. Mona is her mother's daughter and has inherited her difficulty with the sun, and even had a slight touch of sunstroke on the evening of the second day, which Edgar, probably rightly, put down to the fact that Minette had slapped Mona on the cheek, in the back of the car, on the journey down.

'Cheeks afire,' he said, observing his flushed and feverish child. 'You really shouldn't vent your neuroses on your children, Minette.'

And of course Minette shouldn't. Edgar was right. Poor little Mona. It was entirely forgivable for Mona, a child of five, to become fractious and unbiddable in the back of a car, cooped up as she was on a five-hour journey; and entirely unforgivable of the adult Minette, sitting next to her, to be feeling so cross, distraught, nervous and unmaternal that she reacted by slapping. Minette should have, could have diverted: could have sung, could have played Here is the Church, this Little Pig, something, anything, rather than slapped. Cheeks afire! As well they might be. Mona's with upset at her mother's cruel behaviour: Minette's, surely, with shame and sorrow.

Edgar felt the journey was better taken without stops, and that in any case no coffee available on a motorway was worth stopping for. It would be instant, not real. Why hadn't Minette brought a thermos, he enquired, when she ventured to suggest they stopped. Because we don't *own* a thermos, she wanted to cry, in her impossible mood, because you say they're monstrously over-priced, because you say I always break the screw; in any case it's not the coffee I want, it's for you to stop, to recognise our existence, our needs – but she stopped herself in time. That way quarrels lie, and the rare quarrels of Edgar and Minette, breaking out, shatter the neighbourhood, not to mention the children. Well done, Minette.

'Just as well we didn't go to Italy,' said Edgar, on the night of Mona's fever, measuring out, to calm the mother-damaged, fevered cheek, the exact dosage of Junior Aspirin recommended on the back of the packet (and although Minette's doctor once instructed her to quadruple the stated dose, if she wanted it to be effective, Minette knows better than to say so), dissolving it in water, and feeding it to Mona by the spoonful though Minette knows Mona much prefers to suck them – 'if this is what half an hour's English sun does to her.'

Edgar, Minette, Minnie and Mona. Off to Italy, camping, every year for the last six years, even when Mona was a baby. Milan, Venice, Florence, Pisa. Oh

what pleasure, riches, glory, of countryside and town.
This year, Minette had renewed the passports and
replaced the sleeping bags, brought the Melamine
plates and mugs up to quota, checked the Gaz
cylinders, and waited for Edgar to reveal the date,
usually towards the end of July, when he would put
his ethnographical gallery in the hands of an assistant
and they would pack themselves and the tent into the
car, happy families, and set off, as if spontaneously,
into the unknown; but this year the end of July went
and the first week of August, and still Edgar did not
speak, and Minette's employers were betraying a
kind of incredulous restlessness at Minette's apparent
lack of decision, and only then, on August 6, after a
studied absent-mindedness lasting from July 31 to
August 5, did Edgar say 'Of course we can't afford to
go abroad. Business is rock-bottom. I hope you
haven't been wasting any money on unnecessary
equipment?'

'No, of course not,' says Minette. Minette tells many
lies: it is one of the qualities which Edgar least likes in
her. Minette thinks she is safe in this one. Edgar will not
actually count the Melamine plates; nor is he likely to
discern the difference between one old lumpy navy-
blue sleeping bag and another unlumpy new one. 'We
do have the money set aside,' she says cautiously,
hopefully.

'Don't be absurd,' he says. 'We can't afford to drive
the car round the corner, let alone to Venice. It'll only
have sunk another couple of inches since last year,
beneath the weight of crap as much as of tourists. It's

too depressing. Everything's too depressing.' Oh Venice, goodbye Venice, city of wealth and abandon, and human weakness, glorious beneath sulphurous skies. Goodbye Venice, says Minette in her heart, I loved you well. 'So we shan't be having a holiday this year?' she enquires. Tears are smarting in her eyes. She doesn't believe him. She is tired, work has been exhausting. She is an advertising copywriter. He is teasing, surely. He often is. In the morning he will say something different.

'You go on holiday if you want,' he says in the morning. 'I can't. I can't afford a holiday this year. You seem to have lost all sense of reality, Minette. It's that ridiculous place you work in.' And of course he is right. Times are hard. Inflation makes profits and salaries seem ridiculous. Edgar, Minette, Minnie and Mona must adapt with the times. An advertising agency is not noted for the propagation of truth. Those who work in agencies live fantasy lives as to their importance in the scheme of things and their place in a society which in truth despises them. Minette is lucky that someone of his integrity and taste puts up with her. No holiday this year. She will pay the money set aside into a building society, though the annual interest is less than the annual inflation rate. She is resigned.

But the next day, Edgar comes home, having booked a holiday cottage in Kent. A miracle. Friends of his own it, and have had a cancellation. Purest chance. It is the kind of good fortune Edgar always has. If Edgar is one minute late for a train, the train leaves two minutes late.

Now, on the Friday, here they are, Edgar, Minette, Minnie and Mona, installed in this amazing rural paradise of a Kentish hamlet, stone-built, thatched cottage, swifts flying low across the triangular green, the heavy smell of farmyard mixing with the scent of the absurd red roses round the door and the night-stocks in the cottage garden, tired and happy after a day on the beach, with the sun shining and the English Channel blue and gentle, washing upon smooth pebbles.

Mona sleeps, stirs. The night is hot and thundery, ominous. Inflation makes the Monopoly money not so fantastic as it used to be. Minette remarks on it to Edgar.

'Speak for yourself,' he says. Minette recently got a rise, promotion. Edgar is self-employed, of the newly impoverished classes.

They throw to see who goes first. Minette throws a two and three. Minnie, her father's daughter, throws a five and a six. Minnie is twelve, a kindly, graceful child, watchful of her mother, adoring her father, whom she resembles.

Edgar throws a double six. Edgar chooses his token – the iron – and goes first.

Edgar, Minette, Minnie and Mona.

Edgar always wins the toss. Edgar always chooses the iron. (He is as good at housekeeping and cooking as Minette, if not better.) Edgar always wins the game. Minnie always comes second. Minette always comes last. Mona always sleeps. Of such stuff are holidays made.

Monopoly, in truth, bores Minette. She plays for Minnie's sake, to be companionable, and for Edgar's, because it is expected. Edgar likes winning. Who doesn't?

Edgar throws a double, lands on Pentonville Road, and buys it for £60. Minette hands over the card; Minnie receives his money. Edgar throws again, lands on and buys Northumberland Avenue. Minnie throws, lands on Euston Road, next to her father, and buys it for £100. Minette lands on Income Tax, pays £200 into the bank and giggles, partly from nervousness, partly at the ridiculous nature of fate.

'You do certainly have a knack, Minette,' says Edgar, unsmiling. 'But I don't know if it's anything to laugh about.'

Minette stops smiling. The game continues in silence. Minette lands in jail. Upstairs Mona, restless, murmurs and mutters in her sleep. In the distance Minette can hear the crackle of thunder. The windows are open, and the curtains not drawn, in order that Edgar can feel close to the night and nature, and make the most of his holiday. The window squares of blank blackness, set into the white walls, as on some child's painting, frighten Minette. What's outside? Inside, it seems to her, their words echo. The rattle of the dice is loud, loaded with some kind of meaning she'd rather not think about. Is someone else listening, observing?

Mona cries out. Minette gets up. 'I'll go to her,' she says.

'She's perfectly all right,' says Edgar. 'Don't fuss.'

'She might be frightened,' says Minette.

'What of?' enquires Edgar dangerously. 'What is there to be frightened of?' He is irritated by Minette's many fears, especially on holiday, and made angry by the notion that there is anything threatening in nature. Loving silence and isolation himself, he is impatient with those city-dwellers who fear them. Minette and Mona, his feeling is, are city-dwellers by nature, whereas Edgar and Minnie have the souls, the patience, the maturity of the country-dweller, although obliged to live in the town.

'It's rather hot. She's in a strange place,' Minette persists.

'She's in a lovely place,' says Edgar, flatly. 'Of course, she may be having bad dreams.'

Mona is silent again, and Minette is relieved. If Mona is having bad dreams, it is of course Minette's fault, first for having slapped Mona on the cheek, and then, more basically, for having borne a child with such a town-dweller's nature that she suffers from sunburn and sunstroke.

'Mona by name,' says Minette, 'moaner by nature.'

'Takes after her mother,' says Edgar. 'Minette, you forgot to pay £50 last time you landed in jail, so you'll have to stay there until you throw a double.'

'Can't I pay this time round?'

'No you can't,' says Edgar.

They've lost the rule book. All losses in the house are Minette's responsibility, so it is only justice that Edgar's ruling as to the nature of the game shall be accepted. Minette stays in jail.

Mona by name, moaner by nature. It was Edgar named his children, not Minette. Childbirth upset her judgment, made her impossible, or so Edgar said, and she was willing to believe it, struggling to suckle her young under Edgar's alternately indifferent and chiding eye, sore from stitches, trying to decide on a name, and unable to make up her mind, for any name Minette liked, Edgar didn't. For convenience' sake, while searching for a compromise, she referred to her first-born as Mini – such a tiny, beautiful baby – and when Edgar came back unexpectedly with the birth certificate, there was the name Minnie, and Minette gasped with horror, and all Edgar said was, 'But I thought that was what *you* wanted, it's what *you* called her, the State won't wait for ever for *you* to make up your mind; I had to spend all morning in that place and I ought to be in the gallery; I'm exhausted. Aren't you grateful for anything? You've got to get that baby to sleep right through the night somehow before I go mad.' Well, what could she say? Or do? Minnie she was. Minnie Mouse. But in a way it suited her, or at any rate she transcended it, a beautiful loving child, her father's darling, mother's too.

Minette uses Minnie as good Catholics use the saints – as an intercessionary power.

Minnie, see what your father wants for breakfast. Minnie, ask your father if we're going out today.

When Mona was born Minette felt stronger and happier. Edgar, for some reason, was easy and loving. (Minette lost her job: it had been difficult, looking after the six-year-old Minnie, being pregnant again by accident – well, forgetting her pill – still with the house, the shopping and the cleaning to do, and working at the same time: not to mention the washing. They had no washing machine, Edgar feeling, no doubt rightly, that domestic machinery was noisy, expensive, and not really, in the end, labour-saving. Something had to give, and it was Minette's work that did, just in time to save her sanity. The gallery was doing well, and of course Minette's earnings had been increasing Edgar's tax. Or so he believed. She tried to explain that they were taxed separately, but he did not seem to hear, let alone believe.) In any case, sitting up in childbed with her hand in Edgar's, happy for once, relaxed, unemployed – he was quite right, the work did overstrain her, and what was the point – such meaningless, anti-social work amongst such facile, trendy non-people – joking about the new baby's name, she said, listen to her moaning. Perhaps we'd better call her Moaner. Moaner by name, Moaner by nature. Imprudent Minette. And a week later, there he was, with the birth certificate all made out. Mona.

'Good God, woman,' he cried. 'Are you mad? *You* said you wanted Mona. I took *you* at your word. I was doing what *you* wanted.'

'I didn't say that.' She was crying, weak from childbirth, turmoil, the sudden withdrawal of his kindness, his patience.

'Do you want me to produce witnesses?' He was exasperated. She became pregnant again, a year later. She had an abortion. She couldn't cope, Edgar implied that she couldn't, although he never quite said so, so that the burden of the decision was hers and hers alone. But he was right, of course. She couldn't cope. She arranged everything, went to the nursing home by mini-cab, by herself, and came out by mini-cab the next day. Edgar paid half.

Edgar, Minette, Minnie and Mona. Quite enough to be getting on with.

Minette started going to a psychotherapist once a week. Edgar said she had to; she was impossible without. She burned the dinner once or twice – 'how hostile you are,' said Edgar, and after that cooked all meals himself, without reference to anyone's tastes, habits, or convenience. Still, he did know best. Minette, Minnie and Mona adapted themselves splendidly. He was an admirable cook, once you got used to garlic with everything, from eggs to fish.

Presently, Minette went back to work. Well, Edgar could hardly be expected to pay for the psychotherapist, and in any case, electricity and gas bills having doubled even in a household almost without domestic appliances, there was no doubt her earnings came in useful. Presently, Minette was paying all the household bills – and had promotion. She became a group head with twenty people beneath her. She dealt with clients, executives, creative people, secretaries, assistants, with ease and confidence. Compared to Edgar and home, anyone, anything was easy. But that was only to be expected. Edgar was real life. Advertising agencies – and Edgar was right about this – are make-believe. Shut your eyes, snap your fingers, and presto, there one is, large as life. (That is, if you have the right, superficial, rubbishy attitude to make it happen.) And of course, its employees and contacts can be easily manipulated and modified, as dolls can be, in a doll's house. Edgar was not surprised at Minette's success. It was only to be expected. And she never remembered to turn off the lights, and turned up the central heating much too high, being irritatingly sensitive to cold.

Even tonight, this hot sultry night, with the temperature still lingering in the eighties and lightning crackling round the edges of the sky, she shivers.

'You can't be cold,' he enquires. He is buying a property from Minnie. He owns both Get Out of Jail cards, and has had a bank error in his favour of £200. Minnie is doing nicely, on equal bargaining terms with her father. Minette's in jail again.

'It's just so dark out there,' she murmurs.

'Of course it is,' he said. 'It's the country. You miss the town, don't you?' It is an accusation, not a statement.

The cottage is on a hillside: marsh above and below, interrupting the natural path from the summit to the valley. The windows are open front and back as if to offer least interruption, throwing the house and its inhabitants open to the path of whatever forces flow from the top to the bottom of hills. Or so Minette suspects. How can she say so? She, the town-dweller, the obfuscate, standing between Edgar and the light of his expectations, his sensitivity to the natural life-forces which flow between the earth and him.

Edgar has green fingers, no doubt about it. See his tomatoes in the window-box of his Museum Street gallery? What a triumph!

'Couldn't we have the windows closed?' she asks.

'What for?' he enquires. 'Do *you* want the windows closed, Minnie?'

Minnie shrugs, too intent on missing her father's hotel on Northumberland Avenue to care one way or the other.

Minnie has a fierce competitive spirit. Edgar, denying his own, marvels at it.

'Why do you want to shut out the night?' Edgar demands.

'I don't,' Minette protests. But she does. Yes, she does.

Mona stirs and whimpers upstairs: Minette wants to go to her, close her windows, stop the dark rose heads nodding, whispering distress, but how can she? It is Minette's turn to throw the dice. Her hand trembles. Another five. Chance. You win £10, second prize in beauty contest.

'Not with your nose in that condition,' says Edgar, and laughs. Minnie and Minette laugh as well. 'And your cheeks the colour of poor Mona's. Still, one is happy to know there is a natural justice.'

A crack of thunder splits the air; one second, two seconds, three seconds – and there's the lightning, double-forked, streaking down to the oak-blurred ridge of hills in front of the house.

'I love storms,' says Edgar. 'It's coming this way.'

'I'll just go and shut Mona's window,' says Minette.

'She's perfectly all right,' says Edgar. 'Stop fussing and for God's sake stay out of jail. You're casting a gloom, Minette. There's no fun in playing if one's the

only one with hotels.' As of course Edgar is, though
Minnie's scattering houses up and down the board.

Minette lands on Community. A £20 speeding fine
or take a Chance. She takes a Chance. Pay £150 in
school fees.

The air remains dry and still. Thunder and lightning,
though monstrously active, remain at their distance, the
other side of the hills. The front door creaks silently
open, of its own volition. Not a whisper of wind – only
the baked parched air.

'Ooh,' squeaks Minnie, agreeably frightened.

Minette is dry-mouthed with terror, staring at the
black beyond the door.

'A visitor,' cries Edgar. 'Come in, come in,' and he
mimes a welcome to the invisible guest, getting to his
feet, hospitably pulling back the empty ladderback
chair at the end of the table. The house is open, after
all, to whoever, whatever, chooses to call, on the way
from the top of the hill to the bottom.

Minette's mouth is open: her eyes appalled. Edgar
sees, scorns, sneers.

'Don't, Daddy,' says Minnie. 'It's spooky,' but Edgar
is not to be stopped.

'Come in,' he repeats. 'Make yourself at home.
Don't stumble like that. Just because you've got no
eyes.'

Minette is on her feet. Monopoly money, taken
up by the first sudden gust of storm wind, flies about
the room. Minnie pursues it, half-laughing, half-
panicking.

Minette tugs her husband's inflexible arm.

'Stop,' she beseeches. 'Don't tease. Don't.' No eyes! Oh, Edgar, Minette, Minnie and Mona, what blindness is there amongst you now? What threat to your existence? An immense peal of thunder crackles, it seems, directly overhead: lightning, both sheet and fork, dims the electric light and achieves a strobe-lighting effect of cosmic vulgarity, blinding and bouncing round the white walls, and now, upon the wind, rain, large-dropped, blows in through open doors and windows.

'Shut them,' shrieks Minette. 'I told you. Quickly! Minnie, come and help – '

'Don't fuss. What does it matter? A little rain. Surely you're not frightened of storms?' enquires Edgar, standing just where he is, not moving, not helping, like some great tree standing up to a torrent. For once Minette ignores him and with Minnie gets door and windows shut. The rain changes its nature, becomes drenching and blinding; their faces and clothes are wet with it. Minnie runs up to Mona's room, to make that waterproof. Still Edgar stands, smiling, staring out of the window at the amazing splitting sky. Only then, as he smiles, does Minette realise what she has done. She has shut the thing, the person with no eyes, in with her family. Even if it wants to go, would of its own accord drift down on its way towards the valley, it can't.

Minette runs to open the back door. Edgar follows, slow and curious.

'Why do you open the back door,' he enquires, 'having insisted on shutting everything else? You're very strange, Minette.'

Wet, darkness, noise, fear make her brave.

'You're the one who's strange. A man with no eyes!' she declares, sharp and brisk as she sometimes is at her office, chiding inefficiency, achieving sense and justice. 'Fancy asking in a man with no eyes. What sort of countryman would do a thing like that? You know nothing about anything, people, country, nature. Nothing.'

I know more than he does, she thinks, in this mad excess of arrogance. I may work in an advertising agency. I may prefer central heating to carrying coals, and a frozen pizza to a fresh mackerel, but I grant the world its dignity. I am aware of what I don't know, what I don't understand, and that's more than you can do. My body moves with the tides, bleeds with the moon, burns in the sun: I, Minette, I am a poor passing fragment of humanity: I obey laws I only dimly understand, but I am aware that the penalty of defying them is at best disaster, at worst death.

Thing with no eyes. Yes. The Taniwha. The Taniwha will get you if you don't look out! The sightless blundering monster of the bush, catching little children who stumble into him, devouring brains, bones, eyes and all. On that wild Australasian shore which my husband does not recognise as country, being composed of sand, shore and palmy forest, rather than of patchworked fields and thatch, lurked a blind and eyeless thing, that's where the Taniwha lives. The Taniwha will get you if you don't watch out! Little Minette, Mona's age, shrieked it at her infant enemies, on her father's instructions. That'll frighten them, he said, full of admonition and care, as ever. They'll stop teasing, leave you alone. Minette's father, tall as a tree, legs like poles. Little Minette's arms clasped round them to the end, wrenched finally apart, to set him free to abandon her, leave her to the Taniwha. The Taniwha will get you if you don't watch out. Wish it on others, what happens to you? Serve you right, with knobs on.

'You know nothing about anything,' she repeats now. 'What country person, after dark, sits with the windows open and invites in invisible strangers? Especially ones who are blind.'

Well, Edgar is angry. Of course he is. He stares at her bleakly. Then Edgar steps out of the back door into the rain, now fitful rather than torrential, and flings himself upon his back on the grass, face turned to the tumultuous heavens, arms outspread, drinking in noise, rain, wind, nature, at one with the convulsing universe.

Minnie joins her mother at the door.

'What's he doing?' she asks, nervous.

'Being at one with nature,' observes Minette, cool and casual for Minnie's benefit. 'He'll get very wet, I'm afraid.'

Rain turns to hail, spattering against the house like machine-gun bullets. Edgar dives for the safety of the house, stands in the kitchen drying his hair with the dish towel, silent, angrier than ever.

'Can't we go on with Monopoly?' beseeches Minnie from the doorway. 'Can't we, Mum? The money's only got a little damp. I've got it all back.'

'Not until your father puts that chair back as it was.'

'What chair, Minette?' enquires Edgar, so extremely annoyed with his wife that he is actually talking to her direct. The rest of the holiday is lost, she knows it.

'The ladderback chair. You asked in something from the night to sit on it,' cries Minette, over the noise of nature, hung now for a sheep as well as a lamb, 'now put it back where it was.'

Telling Edgar what to do? Impudence.

'You are mad,' he says seriously. 'Why am I doomed to marry mad women?' Edgar's first wife Hetty went into a mental home after a year of marriage and never re-emerged. She was a very trying woman, according to Edgar.

Mad? What's mad in a mad world? Madder than the dice, sending Minette to jail, back and back again, sending Edgar racing round the board, collecting money, property, power: pacing Minnie in between the two of them, but always nearer her father than her mother? Minnie, hot on Edgar's heels, learning habits to last a lifetime?

All the same, oddly, Edgar goes to the ladderback chair, left pulled back for its unseen guest, and puts it in its original position, square against the table.

'Stop being so spooky,' cries Minnie, 'both of you.'

Minette wants to say 'and now tell it to go away –' but her mouth won't say the words. It would make it too much there. Acknowledgment is dangerous; it gives body to the insubstantial.

Edgar turns to Minette. Edgar smiles, as a sane person, humouring, smiles at an insane one. And he takes Minette's raincoat from the peg, wet as he already

is, and races off through the wind to see if the car
windows have been properly closed.

Minette is proud of her Bonnie Cashin raincoat. It
cost one hundred and twenty pounds, though she told
Edgar it was fifteen pounds fifty, reduced from twenty-
three pounds. It has never actually been in the rain
before and she fears for its safety. She can't ask Edgar
not to wear it. He would look at her in blank
unfriendliness and say 'But I thought it was a raincoat. You described it as a raincoat. If it's a raincoat,
why can't you use it in the rain? Or were you lying to
me? It isn't a raincoat after all?'

Honestly, she'd rather the coat shrunk than go
through all that. Silly garment to have bought in the
first place: Edgar was quite right. Well, would have
been had he known. Minette sometimes wonders why
she tells so many lies. Her head is dizzy.

The chair at the top of the table seems empty. The
man with no eyes is out of the house: Edgar, coat over
head, can be seen through the rain haze, stumbling past
the front hedge towards the car. Will lightning strike
him? Will he fall dead? No.

If the car windows are open, whose fault? Hers,
Minnie's?

'I wish you'd see that Mona shut the car door after
her.' Her fault, as Mona's mother. 'And why haven't
you woken her? This is a wonderful storm.'

And up he goes to be a better mother to Mona than
Minette will ever be, waking his reluctant, sleep-heavy
younger daughter to watch the storm, taking her on his
knee, explaining the nature and function of electrical

discharge the while: now ignoring Minette's presence entirely. When annoyed with her, which is much of the time, for so many of Minette's attitudes and pretensions irritate Edgar deeply, he chooses to pretend she doesn't exist.

Edgar, Minette, Minnie and Mona, united, watching a storm from a holiday cottage. Happy families.

The storm passes: soon it is like gunfire, flashing and banging on the other side of the hills. The lights go out. A power-line down, somewhere. No one shrieks, not even Mona: it merely, suddenly, becomes dark. But oh how dark the country is.

'Well,' says Edgar presently, 'where are the matches? Candles?'

Where, indeed. Minette gropes, useless, trembling, up and down her silent haunted home. How foolish of Minette, knowing there was a storm coming, knowing (surely!) that country storms meant country power cuts, not to have located them earlier. Edgar finds them; he knew where they were all the time.

They go to bed. Edgar and Minette pass on the stairs. He is silent. He is not talking to her. She talks to him.

'Well,' she says, 'you're lucky. All he did was make the lights go out. The man with no eyes.'

He does not bother to reply. What can be said to a mad woman that's in any way meaningful?

All night Edgar sleeps on the far edge of the double bed, away from her, forbidding even in his sleep. So, away from her, he will sleep for the next four or even five days. Minette lies awake for an hour or so, and finally drifts off into a stunned and unrefreshing sleep.

In the morning she is brisk and smiling for the sake of the children, her voice fluty with false cheer, like some Kensington lady in Harrods Food Hall. Sweeping the floor, before breakfast, she avoids the end of the table, and the ladderback chair. The man with no eyes has gone, but something lingers.

Edgar makes breakfast. He is formal with her in front of the children, silent when they are on their own, deaf to Minette's pleasantries. Presently she falls silent too. He adorns a plate of scrambled eggs with buttercups and adjures the children to eat them. Minette has some vague recollection of reading that buttercups are poisonous: she murmurs something of the sort and Edgar winces, visibly. She says no more.

No harm comes to the children, of course. She must have misremembered. Edgar plans omelette, a buttercup salad and nettle soup for lunch. That will be fun, he says. Live off the land, like we're all going to have to, soon.

Minette and Mona giggle and laugh and shriek, clutching nettles. If you squeeze they don't sting. Minette, giggling and laughing to keep her children company, has a pain in her heart. They love their father. He loves them.

After lunch – omelette with lovely rich fresh farm eggs, though actually the white falls flat and limp in the bowl and Minette knows they are at least ten days old, but also knows better than to say so, buttercup salad, and stewed nettles, much like spinach – Edgar tells the children that the afternoon is to be spent at an iron age settlement, on Cumber Hill. Mona weeps a little, fearing a hilltop alive with iron men, but Minnie explains there will be nothing there – just a few lumps and bumps in the springy turf, burial mounds and old excavations, and a view all round, and perhaps a flint or two to be found.

'Then why are we going?' asks Mona, but no one answers. 'Will there be walking? Will there be cows? I've got a blister.'

'Mona by name, moaner by nature,' remarks Edgar. But which comes first, Minette wonders. Absently, she gives Minnie and Mona packet biscuits. Edgar protests. Artificial sugar, manufactured crap, ruining teeth, digestion, morale. What kind of mother is she?

'But they're hungry,' she wants to say and doesn't, knowing the reply by heart. How can they be? They've just had lunch.

In the car first Mona is sick, then Minnie. They are both easily sick, and neatly, out of the car window. Edgar does not stop. He says, 'You shouldn't have given them those biscuits. I knew this would happen,' but he does slow down.

Edgar, Minette, Minnie and Mona. Biscuits, buttercups and boiled nettles. Something's got to give.

Cumber Hill, skirted by car, is wild and lovely: a smooth turfed hilltop wet from last night's rain, a natural fort, the ground sloping sharply away from the broad summit, where sheep now graze, humped with burial mounds. Here families lived, died, grieved, were happy, fought off invaders, perished: left something of themselves behind, numinous beneath a heavy sky.

Edgar parks the car a quarter of a mile from the footpath which leads through stony farmland to the hill itself, and the tracks which skirt the fortifications. It will be a long walk. Minnie declines to come with them, as is her privilege as her father's daughter. She will sit in the car and wait and listen to the radio. A nature programme about the habits of buzzards, she assures her father.

'We'll be gone a couple of hours,' warns Minette.

'That long? It's only a hill.'

'There'll be lots of interesting things. Flints, perhaps. Even fossils. Are you sure?'

Minnie nods, her eyes blank with some inner determination.

'If she doesn't want to come, Minette,' says Edgar, 'she doesn't. It's her loss.'

It is the first direct remark Edgar has made to Minette all day. Minette is pleased, smiles, lays her hand on his arm. Edgar ignores her gesture. Did she really think his displeasure would so quickly evaporate? Her lack of perception will merely add to its duration.

Their walking sticks lie in the back of the car – Minette's a gnarled fruit-tree bough, Edgar's a traditional blackthorn (antique, with a carved dog's head for a handle, bought for him by Minette on the occasion of his forty-second birthday, and costing too much, he said by five pounds, being twenty pounds) and Minnie's and Mona's being stout but mongrel lengths of branch from some unnamed and undistinguished tree. Edgar hands Mona her stick, takes up his own and sets off. Minette picks up hers and follows behind. So much for disgrace.

Edgar is brilliant against the muted colours of the hill – a tall, long-legged rust-heaped shape, striding in orange holiday trousers and red shirt, leaping from hillock to hillock, rock to rock, black stick slashing against nettle and thistle and gorse. Mona, trotting along beside him, stumpy-legged, navy-anoraked, is a stocky, valiant, enthusiastic little creature, perpetually falling over her stick but declining to relinquish it.

Mona presently falls behind and walks with her mother, whom she finds more sympathetic than her father as to nettle-sting and cow-pats. Her hand is dry and firm in Minette's. Minette takes comfort from it. Soon Edgar, relieved of Mona's presence, is so far ahead as to be a dark shape occasionally bobbing into sight over a mound or out from behind a wall or tree.

'I don't see any iron men,' says Mona. 'Only nettles and sheep mess. And cow splats, where I'm walking. Only I don't see any cows either. I expect they're invisible.'

'All the iron men died long ago.'

'Then why have we come here?'

'To think about things.'

'What things?'

'The past, the present, the future,' replies Minette.

The wind gets up, blowing damply in their faces. The sun goes in; the hills lose what colour they had. All is grey, the colour of depression. Winter is coming, thinks Minette. Another season, gone. Clouds, descending, drift across the hills, lie in front of them in misty swathes. Minette can see neither back nor forward. She is frightened: Edgar is nowhere to be seen.

'There might be savage cows in there,' says Mona, 'where we can't see.'

'Wait,' she says to Mona, 'wait,' and means to run ahead to find Edgar and bring him back; but Edgar appears again as if at her will, within earshot, off on a parallel path to theirs, which will take him on yet another circumnavigation of the lower-lying fortifications.

'I'll take Mona back to the car,' she calls. He looks astonished.

'Why?'

He does not wait for her answer: he scrambles over a hillock and disappears.

'Because,' she wants to call after him, 'because I am forty, alone and frightened. Because my period started yesterday, and I have a pain. Because my elder child sits alone in a car in mist and rain, and my younger one stands grizzling on a misty hilltop, shivering with fright, afraid of invisible things, and cold. Because if I stay a minute longer I will lose my way and wander here for ever. Because battles were fought on this hilltop, families who were happy died and something remains behind, by comparison with which the Taniwha, sightless monster of the far-off jungle, those white and distant shores, is a model of goodwill.'

Minette says nothing: in any case he has gone.

'Let's get back to the car,' she says to Mona.

'Where is it?' enquires Mona, pertinently.

'We'll find it.'

'Isn't Daddy coming?'

'He'll be coming later.'

Something of Minette's urgency communicates itself to Mona: or some increasing fear of the place itself. Mona leads the way back, without faltering, without complaint, between nettles, over rocks, skirting the barbed-wire fence, keeping a safe distance from the cows, at last made flesh, penned up on the other side of the fence.

The past. Minette at Mona's age, leading her weeping mother along a deserted beach to their deserted cottage. Minette's father, prime deserter. Man with no eyes for Minette's distress, her mother's despair. Little Minette with her arms clutched rigidly round her father's legs, finally disentangled by determined adult arms. Whose? She does not know. Her father walking off with someone else, away from the wailing Minette, his daughter, away from the weeping mother, his wife. Later, it was found that one of Minette's fingers was broken. He never came back. Sunday outings, thereafter, just the two of them, Minette and mother, valiantly striving for companionable pleasure, but what use is a three-legged stool with two legs? That's what they were.

The present? Mist, clouds, in front, behind; the wind blowing her misery back in her teeth. Minette and Mona stumble, hold each other up. The clouds part. There's the road: there's the car. Only a few hundred yards. There is Minnie, red hair gleaming, half-asleep, safe.

'England home and safety!' cries Minette, ridiculous, and with this return to normality, however baffling, Mona sits down on the ground and refuses to go another step, and has to be entreated, cajoled and bluffed back to the car.

'Where's Daddy?' complains Minnie. It is her children's frequent cry. That and 'Are you all right, Mummy?'

'We got tired and came back,' says Minette.

'I suppose he'll be a long time. He always is.'

Minette looks at her watch. Half-past four. They've been away an hour and a half.

'I should say six o'clock.' Edgar's walks usually last for three hours. Better resign herself to this than to exist in uneasy expectation.

'What will we do?'

'Listen to the radio. Read. Think. Talk. Wait. It's very nice up here. There's a view.'

'I've been looking at it for three hours,' says Minnie, resigned. 'Oh well.'

'But I'm hungry,' says Mona. 'Can I have an iced lolly?'

'Idiot,' says Minnie to her sister. 'Idiot child.'

There is nothing in sight except the empty road, hills, mist. Minette can't drive. Edgar thinks she would be a danger to herself and others if she learned. If there was a village within walking distance she would take the children off for tea, but there is nothing. She and Minnie consult the maps and discover this sad fact. Mona, fortunately, discovers an ant's nest. Minnie and Minette play I-Spy.

Minette, busy, chirpy, stands four square between her children and desolation.

Five o'clock. Edgar reappears, emerging brilliantly out of the mist, from an unexpected direction, smiling satisfaction.

'Wonderful,' he says. 'I can't think why you went back, Minette.'

'Mummy was afraid of the cows,' says Mona.

'Your mother is afraid of everything,' says Edgar. 'I'm afraid she and nature don't get along together.'

They pile back into the car and off they go. Edgar starts to sing, 'One man went to mow.' They all join in. Happy families. A cup of tea, thinks Minette. How I would love a cup of immoral tea, a plate of fattening sandwiches, another of ridiculous iced cakes, in one of the beamed and cosy tea-shops in which the Kentish villages abound. How long since Minette had a cup of tea? How many years?

Edgar does not like tea – does not approve of eating between meals. Tea is a drug, he says: it is the rot of the English: it is a laughable substance, a false stimulant, of no nutritive value whatsoever, lining the stomach with tannin. Tea! Minette, do you want a cup of tea? Of course not. Edgar is right. Minette's mother died of stomach cancer, after a million comforting cups. Perhaps they did instead of sex? The singing stops. In the back of the car, Minette keeps silent; presently cries silently, when Mona, exhausted, falls asleep. Last night was disturbed.

The future? Like the past, like the present. Little girls who lose their fathers cry all their lives. Hard to blame

Edgar for her tears: no doubt she makes Edgar the cause of them. He says so often enough. Mona and Minette shall not lose their father, she is determined on it. Minette will cry now and for ever, so that Minnie and Mona can grow up to laugh – though no doubt their laughter, as they look back, will be tinged with pity, at best, and derision, at worst, for a mother who lives as theirs did. Minnie and Mona, saved from understanding.

I am of the lost generation, thinks Minette, one of millions. Inter-leaving, blotting up the miseries of the past, to leave the future untroubled. I would be happier dead, but being alive, of necessity, might as well make myself useful. She sings softly to the sleeping Mona, chats brightly to Minnie.

Edgar, Minette, Minnie and Mona. Nothing gives.

That night, when Mona is in bed, and Minnie has set up the Monopoly board, Edgar moves as of instinct into the ladderback chair, and Minette plays Monopoly, Happy Families, with the Man with no Eyes.

1977

Angel, All Innocence

There is a certain kind of unhappiness, experienced by a certain kind of woman married to a certain kind of man, which is timeless: outrunning centuries, interweaving generations, perpetuating itself from mother to daughter, feeding off the wet eyes of the puzzled girl, gaining fresh strength from the dry eyes of the old woman she will become – who, looking back on her past, remembers nothing of love except tears and the pain in the heart which must be endured, in silence, in case the heart stops altogether.

Better for it to stop, now.

Angel, waking in the night, hears sharp footsteps in the empty attic above and wants to wake Edward. She moves her hand to do so, but then stills it for fear of making him angry. Easier to endure in the night the nightmare terror of ghosts than the day-long silence of Edward's anger.

The footsteps, little and sharp, run from a point above the double bed in which Angel and Edward lie, she awake, he sleeping, to a point somewhere above the chest of drawers by the door; they pause briefly, then run back again, tap-tap, clickety-click. There comes another pause and the sound of pulling and shuffling across the floor; and then the sequence repeats itself, once, twice. Silence. The proper unbroken silence of the night.

Too real, too clear, for ghosts. The universe is not magic. Everything has an explanation. Rain, perhaps? Hardly. Angel can see the moon shine through the drawn blind, and rain does not fall on moonlit nights. Perhaps, then, the rain of past days collected in some blocked gutter, to finally splash through on to the rolls of wallpaper and pots of paint on the attic floor, sounding like footsteps through some trick of domestic acoustics. Surely! Angel and Edward have not been living in the house for long. The attic is still unpainted, and old plaster drops from disintegrating laths. Edward will get round to it sooner or later. He prides himself on his craftsman's skills, and Angel, a year married, has learned to wait and admire, subduing impatience in herself. Edward is a painter – of pictures, not houses – and not long out of art school, where he won many prizes. Angel is the lucky girl he has loved and married. Angel's father paid for the remote country house, where now they live in solitude and where Edward can develop his talents, undisturbed by the ugliness of the city, with Angel, his inspiration, at his side. Edward, as it happened, consented to the gift unwillingly, and for Angel's sake rather than his own. Angel's father Terry writes thrillers and settled a large sum upon his daughter in her childhood, thus avoiding death duties and the anticipated gift tax. Angel kept the fact hidden

from Edward until after they were married. He'd
thought her an ordinary girl about Chelsea, sometime
secretary, sometime barmaid, sometime artist's model.

Angel, between jobs, did indeed take work as an
artist's model. That was how Edward first clapped eyes
upon her; Angel, all innocence, sitting nude upon her
plinth, fair curly hair glinting under strong lights, large
eyes closed beneath stretched blue-veined lids, strong
breasts pointed upwards, stubby pale brush irritatingly
and coyly hidden behind an angle of thigh that both
gave Angel cramps and spoiled the pose for the
students. So they said.

'If you're going to be an exhibitionist,' as Edward
complained to her later in the coffee bar, 'at least don't
be coy about it.' He took her home to his pad, that
handsome, dark-eyed, smiling young man, and wooed
her with a nostalgic Sinatra record left behind by its
previous occupant; half mocking, half sincere, he sang
love words into her pearly ear, his warm breath therein
stirring her imagination, and the gentle occasional nip
of his strong teeth in its flesh promising passion and
pain beyond belief. Angel would not take off her
clothes for him: he became angry and sent her home
in a taxi without her fare. She borrowed from her
flatmate at the other end. She cried all night, and the
next day, sitting naked on her plinth, had such swollen
eyelids as to set a student or two scratching away to
amend the previous day's work. But she lowered her
thigh, as a gesture of submission, and felt a change in
the studio ambience from chilly spite to warm approval, and she knew Edward had forgiven her.

Though she offered herself to multitudes, Edward had forgiven her.

'I don't mind you being an exhibitionist,' Edward said to her in the coffee bar, 'in fact that rather turns me on, but I do mind you being coy. You have a lot to learn, Angel.' By that time Angel's senses were so aroused, her limbs so languid with desire, her mind so besotted with his image, that she would have done whatever Edward wished, in public or in private. But he rose and left the coffee bar, leaving her to pay the bill.

Angel cried a little, and was comforted by and went home with Edward's friend Tom, and even went to bed with him, which made her feel temporarily better, but which she was to regret for ever.

'I don't mind you being a whore,' Edward said before the next studio session, 'but can't you leave my friends alone?'

It was a whole seven days of erotic torment for Angel before Edward finally spent the night with her: by that time her thigh hung loosely open in the studio. Let anyone see. Anyone. She did not care. The job was coming to an end anyway. Her new one as secretary in a solicitor's office began on the following Monday. In the nick of time, just as she began to think that life and love were over, Edward brought her back to their remembrance. 'I love you,' he murmured in Angel's ear. 'Exhibitionist slut, typist, I don't care. I still love you.'

Tap-tap, go the footsteps above, starting off again: clickety-click. Realer than real. No, water never

sounded like that. What then? Rats? No. Rats scutter
and scamper and scrape. There were rats in the barn in
which Angel and Edward spent a camping holiday
together. Their tent had blown away: they'd been
forced to take refuge in the barn. All four of them.
Edward, Angel, Tom and his new girlfriend Ray.
Angel missed Edward one night after they all stumbled
back from the pub to the barn, and searching for him in
the long grass beneath an oak tree, found him in tight
embrace with Ray.

'Don't tell me you're hysterical as well as everything
else,' complained Edward. 'You're certainly irrational.
You went to bed with Tom, after all.'

'But that was before.'

Ah, before, so much before. Before the declarations
of love, the abandoning of all defence, all prudence, the
surrendering of common sense to faith, the parcelling
up and handing over of the soul into apparent safe-
keeping. And if the receiving hands part, the trusted
fingers lose their grip, by accident or by design, why
then, one's better dead.

Edward tossed his Angel's soul into the air and
caught it with his casual hands.

'But if it makes you jealous,' he said, 'why I won't
. . . Do you want to marry me? Is that it? Would it
make you happier?'

What would it look like when they came to write his
biography? Edward Holst, the famous painter, married
at the age of twenty-four – to what? Artist's model,
barmaid, secretary, crime-writer's daughter? Or exhibitionist, whore, hysteric? Take your choice. Whatever

makes the reader happiest, explains the artist in the simplest terms, makes the most successful version of a life. Crude strokes and all.

'Edward likes to keep his options open,' said Tom, but would not explain his remark any further. He and Ray were witnesses at the secular wedding ceremony. Angel thought she saw Edward nip Ray's ear as they all formally kissed afterwards, then thought she must have imagined it.

This was his overture of love: turning to Angel in the dark warmth of the marriage bed, Edward's teeth would seek her ear and nibble the tender flesh, while his hand travelled down to open her thighs. Angel never initiated their love-making. No. Angel waited, patiently. She had tried once or twice, in the early days, letting her hand roam over his sleeping body, but Edward not only failed to respond, but was thereafter cold to her for days on end, sleeping carefully on his side of the bed, until her penance was paid and he lay warm against her again.

Edward's love made flowers bloom, made the house rich and warm, made water taste like wine. Edward, happy, surrounded Angel with smiles and soft encouragement. He held her soul with steady hands. Edward's anger came unexpectedly, out of nowhere, or nowhere that Angel could see. Yesterday's permitted remark, forgiven fault, was today's outrage. To remark on the weather to break an uneasy silence, might be seen as evidence of a complaining nature: to be reduced to tears by his first unexpected biting remark, further fuel for his grievance.

Edward, in such moods, would go to his studio
and lock the door, and though Angel (soon learning
that to weep outside the door or beat against it,
moaning and crying and protesting, would merely
prolong his anger and her torment) would go out to
the garden and weed or dig or plant as if nothing
were happening, would feel Edward's anger seeping
out from under the door, darkening the sun, poison-
ing the earth; or at any rate spoiling her fingers in
relation to the earth, so that they trembled and made
mistakes and nothing grew.

The blind shakes. The moon goes behind a cloud.
Tap, tap, overhead. Back and forth. The wind? No.
Don't delude yourself. Nothing of this world. A ghost.
A haunting. A woman. A small, desperate, busy
woman, here and not here, back and forth, out of
her time, back from the grave, ill-omened, bringing
grief and ruin: a message that nothing is what it seems,
that God is dead and the forces of evil abroad and
unstoppable. Does Angel hear, or not hear?

Angel through her fear, wants to go to the bathroom. She is three months pregnant. Her bladder is
weak. It wakes her in the night, crying out its need, and
Angel, obeying, will slip cautiously out of bed, trying
not to wake Edward. Edward needs unbroken sleep if
he is to paint well the next day. Edward, even at the
best of times, suspects that Angel tossing and turning,
and moaning in her sleep, as she will, wakes him on
purpose to annoy.

Angel has not yet told Edward that she is pregnant.
She keeps putting it off. She has no real reason to

believe he does not want babies: but he has not said he does want them, and to assume that Edward wants what other people want is dangerous.

Angel moans aloud: afraid to move, afraid not to move, afraid to hear, afraid not to hear. So the child Angel lay awake in her little white bed, listening to her mother moaning, afraid to move, afraid not to move, to hear or not to hear. Angel's mother was a shoe-shop girl who married the new assistant manager after a six-week courtship. That her husband went on to make a fortune, writing thrillers that sold by the million, was both Dora's good fortune and tragedy. She lived comfortably enough on alimony, after all, in a way she could never have expected, until dying by mistake from an overdose of sleeping pills. After that Angel was brought up by a succession of her father's mistresses and au-pairs. Her father Terry liked Edward, that was something, or at any rate he had been relieved at his appearance on the scene. He had feared an element of caution in Angel's soul: that she might end up married to a solicitor or stockbroker. And artists were at least creative, and an artist such as Edward Holst might well end up rich and famous. Terry had six Holst canvases on his walls to hasten the process. Two were of his daughter, nude, thigh slackly falling away from her stubby fair bush. Angel, defeated – as her mother had been defeated. 'I love you, Dora, but you must understand. I am not *in* love with you.' As I'm in love with Helen, Audrey, Rita, whoever it was: off to meetings, parties, off on his literary travels,

looking for fresh copy and new backgrounds, en-
countering always someone more exciting, more
interesting, than an ageing ex shoe-shop assistant.
Why couldn't Dora understand? Unreasonable of her
to suffer, clutching the wretched Angel to her
alarmingly slack bosom. Could he, Terry, really be
the only animation of her flesh? There was a sickness
in her love, clearly; unaccompanied as it was by the
beauty which lends grace to importunity.

Angel had her mother's large, sad eyes. The reproach
in them was in-built. Better Dora's heart had stopped
(she'd thought it would: six months pregnant, she
found Terry in the housemaid's bed. She, Dora,
mistress of servants! What bliss!) and the embryo Angel
never emerged to the light of day.

The noise above Angel stops. Ghosts! What nonsense! A fallen lath grating and rattling in the wind.
What else?

Angel regains her courage, slips her hand out from
beneath Edward's thigh preparatory to leaving the bed
for the bathroom. She will turn on all the lights and
run. Edward wakes; sits up.

'What's that? What in God's name's that?'

'I can't hear anything,' says Angel, all innocence.
Nor can she, not now. Edward's displeasure to contend
with now; worse than the universe rattling its chains.

'Footsteps, in the attic. Are you deaf? Why didn't
you wake me?'

'I thought I imagined it.'

But she can hear them, once again, as if with his ears.
The same pattern across the floor and back. Footsteps

or heartbeats. Quicker and quicker now, hastening with the terror and tension of escape.

Edward, unimaginably brave, puts on his slippers, grabs a broken banister (five of these on the landing – one day soon, some day, he'll get round to mending them – he doesn't want some builder, paid by Angel, bungling the job) and goes on up to the attic. Angel follows behind. He will not let her cower in bed. Her bladder aches. She says nothing about that. How can she? Not yet. Not quite yet. Soon. 'Edward, I'm pregnant.' She can't believe it's true, herself. She feels a child, not a woman.

'Is there someone there?'

Edward's voice echoes through the three dark attic rooms. Silence. He gropes for and switches on the light. Empty, derelict rooms: plaster falling, laths hanging, wallpaper peeling. Floorboards broken. A few cans of paint, a pile of wallpaper rolls, old newspapers. Nothing else.

'It could have been mice,' says Edward, doubtfully.

'Can't you hear it?' asks Angel, terrified. The sound echoes in her ears: footsteps clattering over a pounding heart. But Edward can't, not any more.

'Don't start playing games,' he murmurs, turning back to warmth and bed. Angel scuttles down before him, into the bathroom; the noise in her head fades. A few drops of urine tinkle into the bowl.

Edward lies awake in bed: Angel can feel his wakefulness, his increasing hostility towards her, before she is so much as back in the bedroom.

'Your bladder's very weak, Angel,' he complains. 'Something else you inherited from your mother?'

Something else, along with what? Suicidal tendencies, alcoholism, a drooping bosom, a capacity for being betrayed, deserted and forgotten?

Not forgotten by me, Mother. I don't forget. I love you. Even when my body cries out beneath the embraces of this man, this lover, this husband, and my mouth forms words of love, promises of eternity, still I don't forget. I love you, Mother.

'I don't know about my mother's bladder,' murmurs Angel rashly.

'Now you're going to keep me awake all night,' says Edward. 'I can feel it coming. You know I've nearly finished a picture.'

'I'm not going to say a word,' she says, and then, fulfilling his prophecy, sees fit to add, 'I'm pregnant.'

Silence. Stillness. Sleep?

No, a slap across nostrils, eyes mouth. Edward has never hit Angel before. It is not a hard slap: it contains the elements of a caress.

'Don't even joke about it,' says Edward, softly.

'But I am pregnant.'

Silence. He believes her. Her voice made doubt impossible.

'How far?' Edward seldom asks for information. It is an act which infers ignorance, and Edward likes to know more than anyone else in the entire world.

'Three and a half months.'

He repeats the words, incredulous.

'Too far gone to do anything,' says Angel, knowing now why she did not tell Edward earlier, and the knowledge making her voice cold and hard. Too far gone for the abortion he will most certainly want her to have. So much for the fruits of love. Love? What's love? Sex, ah, that's another thing. Love has babies: sex has abortions.

But Angel will turn sex into love – yes, she will – seizing it by the neck, throttling it till it gives up and takes the weaker path. Love! Edward is right to be frightened, right to hate her.

'I hate you,' he says, and means it. 'You mean to destroy me.'

'I'll make sure it doesn't disturb your nights,' says Angel, Angel of the bristly fair bush, 'if that's what you're worrying about. And you won't have to support it. I do that, anyway. Or my father does.'

Well, how dare she! Angel, not nearly as nice as she thought. Soft-eyed, vicious Angel.

Slap, comes the hand again, harder. Angel screams, he shouts; she collapses, crawls about the floor – he spurns her, she begs forgiveness; he spits his hatred, fear, and she her misery. If the noise above continues, certainly no one hears it, there is so much going on below. The rustlings of the night erupting into madness. Angel is suddenly quiet, whimpering, lying on the floor; she squirms. At first Edward thinks she is acting, but her white lips and taloned fingers convince him that something is wrong with her body and not just her mind. He gets her back on the bed and rings the doctor. Within an hour Angel finds herself in a hospital with a suspected ectopic pregnancy. They delay the operation and the pain subsides; just one of those things, they shrug. Edward has to interrupt his painting the next afternoon to collect her from the hospital.

'What was it? Hysteria?' he enquires.

'I dare say!'

'Well, you had a bad beginning, what with your mother and all,' he concedes, kissing her nose, nibbling her earlobe. It is forgiveness; but Angel's eyes remain unusually cold. She stays in bed, after Edward has left it and gone back to his studio, although the floors remain unswept and the dishes unwashed.

Angel does not say what is in her mind, what she knows to be true. That he is disappointed to see both her and the baby back, safe and sound. He had hoped the baby would die, or failing that, the mother would die and the baby with her. He is pretending forgiveness, while he works out what to do next.

In the evening the doctor comes to see Angel. He is a slight man with a sad face: his eyes, she thinks, are kind behind his pebble glasses. His voice is slow and gentle. I expect his wife is happy, thinks Angel, and actually envies her. Some middle-aged, dowdy, provincial doctor's wife, envied by Angel! Rich, sweet, young and pretty Angel. The efficient secretary, lovable barmaid, and now the famous artist's wife! Once, for two rash weeks, even an art school model.

The doctor examines her, then discreetly pulls down her nightie to cover her breasts and moves the sheet up to cover her crotch. If he were my father, thinks Angel, he would not hang my naked portrait on his wall for the entertainment of his friends. Angel had not known until this moment that she minded.

'Everything's doing nicely inside there,' says the doctor. 'Sorry to rush you off like that, but we can't take chances.'

Ah, to be looked after. Love. That's love. The doctor shows no inclination to go.

'Perhaps I should have a word with your husband,' he suggests. He stands at the window gazing over daffodils and green fields. 'Or is he very busy?'

'He's painting,' says Angel. 'Better not disturb him now. He's had so many interruptions lately, poor man.'

'I read about him in the Sunday supplement,' says the doctor.

'Well, don't tell him so. He thought it vulgarised his work.'

'Did you think that?'

Me? Does what I think have anything to do with anything?

'I thought it was quite perceptive, actually,' says Angel, and feels a surge of good humour. She sits up in bed.

'Lie down,' he says. 'Take things easy. This is a large house. Do you have any help? Can't afford it?'

'It's not that. It's just why should I expect some other woman to do my dirty work?'

'Because she might like doing it and you're pregnant, and if you can afford it, why not?'

'Because Edward doesn't like strangers in the house. And what else have I got to do with my life? I might as well clean as anything else.'

'It's isolated out here,' he goes on. 'Do you drive?'

'Edward needs peace to paint,' says Angel. 'I do drive but Edward has a thing about women drivers.'

'You don't miss your friends?'

'After you're married,' says Angel, 'you seem to lose contact. It's the same for everyone, isn't it?'

'Um,' says the doctor. And then, 'I haven't been in this house for fifteen years. It's in a better state now than it was then. The house was divided into flats, in those days. I used to visit a nice young woman who had the attic floor. Just above this. Four children, and the roof leaked; a husband who spent his time drinking cider in the local pub and only came home to beat her.'

'Why did she stay?'

'How can such women leave? How do they afford it? Where do they go? What happens to the children?' His voice is sad.

'I suppose it's money that makes the difference. With money, a woman's free,' says Angel, trying to believe it.

'Of course,' says the doctor. 'But she loved her husband. She couldn't bring herself to see him for what he was. Well, it's hard. For a certain kind of woman, at any rate.'

Hard, indeed, if he has your soul in his safe-keeping, to be left behind at the bar, in the pub, or in some other woman's bed, or in a seat in the train on his literary travels. Careless!

'But it's not like that for you, is it?' says the doctor calmly. 'You have money of your own, after all.'

Now how does he know that? Of course, the Sunday supplement article.

'No one will read it,' wept Angel, when Edward

looked up, stony-faced from his first perusal of the fashionable columns. 'No one will notice. It's tucked away at the very bottom.'

So it was. 'Edward's angelic wife Angel, daughter of best-selling crime-writer Terry Toms, has smoothed the path upwards, not just with the soft smiles our cameraman has recorded, but by enabling the emergent genius to forswear the cramped and inconvenient, if traditional, artist's garret for a sixteenth-century farm-house in greenest Gloucestershire. It is interesting, moreover, to ponder whether a poor man would have been able to develop the white-on-white tech-niques which have made Holst's work so noticeable: or whether the sheer price of paint these days would not have deterred him.'

'Edward, I didn't say a word to that reporter, not a word,' she said, when the ice showed signs of cracking, days later.

'What are you talking about?' he asked, turning slow, unfriendly eyes upon her.

'The article. I know it's upset you. But it wasn't my fault.'

'Why should a vulgar article in a vulgar newspaper upset me?'

And the ice formed over again, thicker than ever. But he went to London for two days, presumably to arrange his next show, and on his return casually mentioned that he'd seen Ray while he was there.

Angel had cleaned, baked, and sewed curtains in his absence, hoping to soften his heart towards her on his return: and lay awake all the night he was away, the fear of his infidelity so agonising as to make her contemplate suicide, if only to put an end to it. She could not ask for reassurance. He would throw the fears so neatly back at her. 'Why do you think I should want to sleep with anyone else? Why are you so guilty? Because that's what you'd do if you were away from me?'

Ask for bread and be given stones. Learn self-sufficiency: never show need. Little, tough Angel of the soft smiles, hearing some other woman's footsteps in the night, crying for another's grief. Well, who wants a soul, tossed here and there by teasing hands, over-bruised and over-handled. Do without it!

Edward came home from London in a worse mood than he'd left, shook his head in wondering stupefaction at his wife's baking – 'I thought you said we were cutting down on carbohydrates' – and shut himself into his studio for twelve hours, emerging just once to say – 'Only a mad woman would hang curtains in an artist's studio, or else a silly rich girl playing at artist's wife, and in public at that' – and thrusting the new curtains back into her arms, vanished inside again.

Angel felt that her mind was slowing up, and puzzled over the last remark for some time before realising that Edward was still harking back to the Sunday supplement article.

'I'll give away the money if you like,' she pleaded through the keyhole. 'If you'd rather. And if you want not to be married to me I don't mind.' That was before she was pregnant.

Silence.

Then Edward emerged laughing, telling her not to be so ridiculous, bearing her off to bed, and the good times were restored. Angel sang about the house, forgot her pill, and got pregnant.

'You have money of your own, after all,' says the doctor.

'You're perfectly free to come and go.'

'I'm pregnant,' says Angel. 'The baby has to have a father.'

'And your husband's happy about the baby?'

'Oh yes!' says Angel. 'Isn't it a wonderful day!'

And indeed today the daffodils nod brightly under a clear sky. So far, since first they budded and bloomed, they have been obliged to droop beneath the weight of rain and mist. A disappointing spring. Angel had hoped to see the countryside leap into energy and colour, but life returned only slowly, it seemed, struggling to surmount the damage of the past: cold winds and hard frosts, unseasonably late. 'Or at any rate,' adds Angel, softly, unheard, as the doctor goes, 'he *will* be happy about the baby.'

Angel hears no more noises in the night for a week or so. There had been misery in the attic rooms, and the misery had ceased. Good times can wipe out bad. Surely!

Edward sleeps soundly and serenely: she creeps from bed to bathroom without waking him. He is kind to her and even talkative, on any subject, that is, except that of her pregnancy. If it were not for the doctor and her stay in the hospital, she might almost think she was imagining the whole thing. Edward complains that

Angel is getting fat, as if he could imagine no other cause for it but greed. She wants to talk to someone about hospitals, confinements, layettes, names – but to whom?

She tells her father on the telephone – 'I'm pregnant.'

'What does Edward say?' asks Terry, cautiously.

'Nothing much,' admits Angel.

'I don't suppose he does.'

'There's no reason *not* to have a baby,' ventures Angel.

'I expect he rather likes to be the centre of attention.' It is the nearest Terry has ever got to a criticism of Edward.

Angel laughs. She is beyond believing that Edward could ever be jealous of her, ever be dependent upon her.

'Nice to hear you happy, at any rate,' says her father wistfully. His twenty-year-old girlfriend has become engaged to a salesman of agricultural machinery, and although she has offered to continue the relationship the other side of marriage, Terry feels debased and used, and was obliged to break off the liaison. He has come to regard his daughter's marriage to Edward in a romantic light. The young bohemians!

'My daughter was an art school model before she married Edward Holst . . . you've heard of him? It's a real Rembrandt and Saskia affair.' He even thinks lovingly of Dora: if only she'd understood, waited for youth to wear itself out. Now he's feeling old and perfectly capable of being faithful to an ex shoe-shop assistant. If only she weren't dead and gone!

An art school model. Those two weeks! Why had she done it? What devil wound up her works and set poor Angel walking in the wrong direction? It was in her nature, surely, as it was in her mother's to follow the paths to righteousness, fully clothed.

Nightly, Edward studied her naked body, kissing her here, kissing her there, parting her legs. Well, marriage! But now I'm pregnant, now I'm pregnant. Oh, be careful. That hard lump where my soft belly used to be. Be careful! Silence, Angel. Don't speak of it. It will be the worse for you and your baby if you do.

Angel knows it.

Now Angel hears the sound of lovemaking up in the empty attic, as she might hear it in hotels in foreign lands. The couplings of strangers in an unknown tongue – only the cries and breathings universal, recognisable anywhere.

The sounds chill her: they do not excite her. She thinks of the mother of four who lived in this house with her drunken, violent husband. Was that what kept you by his side? The chains of fleshly desire? Was it the thought of the night that got you through the perils of the day?

What indignity, if it were so.

Oh, I imagine it. I, Angel, half-mad in my unacknowledged pregnancy, my mind feverish, and the doctor's anecdotes feeding the fever – I imagine it! I must!

Edward wakes.

'What's that noise?'

'What noise?'

'Upstairs.'

'I don't hear anything.'

'You're deaf.'

'What sort of noise?'

But Edward sleeps again. The noise fades, dimly. Angel hears the sound of children's voices. Let it be a girl, dear Lord, let it be a girl.

'Why do you want a girl?' asks the doctor, on Angel's fourth monthly visit to the clinic.

'I'd love to dress a girl,' says Angel vaguely, but what she means is, if it's a girl, Edward will not be so – what is the word? – hardly jealous, difficult perhaps. Dreadful. Yes, dreadful.

Bright-eyed Edward: he walks with Angel now – long walks up and over stiles, jumping streams, leaping stones. Young Edward. She has begun to feel rather old, herself.

'I am a bit tired,' she says, as they set off one night for their moon-lit walk.

He stops, puzzled.

'Why are you tired?'

'Because I'm pregnant,' she says, in spite of herself.

'Don't start that again,' he says, as if it were hysteria on her part. Perhaps it is.

That night, he opens her legs so wide she thinks she will burst. 'I love you,' he murmurs in her nibbled ear, 'Angel, I love you. I do love you.' Angel feels the familiar surge of response, the holy gratitude, the willingness to die, to be torn apart if that's what's required. And then it stops. It's gone. Evaporated! And in its place, a new strength. A chilly icicle of non-response, wonderful, cheerful. No. It isn't right; it isn't what's required: on the contrary. 'I love you,' she says in return, as usual; but crossing her fingers in her mind, forgiveness for a lie. Please God, dear God, save me, help me save my baby. It is not me he loves, but my baby he hates: not me he delights in, but the pain he causes me, and knows he does. He does not wish to take root in me: all he wants to do is root my baby out. I don't love him. I never have. It is sickness. I must get well. Quickly.

'Not like that,' says Angel, struggling free – bold, unkind, prudish Angel – rescuing her legs. 'I'm pregnant. I'm sorry, but I am pregnant.'

Edward rolls off her, withdraws.

'Christ, you can be a monster. A real ball-breaker.'

'Where are you going?' asks Angel, calm and curious. Edward is dressing. Clean shirt; cologne. Cologne!

'To London.'

'Why?'

'Where I'm appreciated.'

'Don't leave me alone. Please.' But she doesn't mean it.

'Why not?'

'I'm frightened. Here alone at night.'

'Nothing ever frightened you.' Perhaps he is right.

Off he goes; the car breaking open the silence of the night. It closes again. Angel is alone.

Tap, tap, tap, up above. Starting up as if on signal. Back and forward. To the attic bed which used to be, to the wardrobe which once was; the scuffle of the suitcase on the floor. Goodbye. I'm going. I'm frightened here. The house is haunted. Someone upstairs, downstairs. Oh, women everywhere, don't think your misery doesn't seep into walls, creep downstairs, and then upstairs again. Don't think it will ever be done with, or that the good times wipe it out. They don't.

Angel feels her heart stop and start again. A neurotic symptom, her father's doctor had once said. It will get better, he said, when she's married and has babies. Everything gets better for women when they're married with babies. It's their natural state. Angel's heart stops all the same, and starts again, for good or bad.

Angel gets out of bed, slips on her mules with their sharp little heels, and goes up the attic stairs. Where does she find the courage? The light, reflected up from the hallway, is dim. The noise from the attic stops. Angel hears only – what? – the rustling noise of old newspapers in a fresh wind. That stops, too. As if a film were now running without sound. And coming down towards Angel, a small, tired woman in a nightie, slippers silent on the stairs, stopping to stare at Angel as Angel stares at her. Her face marked by bruises.

'How can I see that,' wonders Angel, now unafraid, 'since there isn't any light?'

She flicks on the switch, hand trembling, and in the light, as she'd known, there is nothing to be seen except the empty stairs and the unmarked dust upon them.

Angel goes back to the bedroom and sits on the bed.

'I saw a ghost,' she tells herself, calmly enough. Then fear reasserts itself: panic at the way the universe plays tricks. Quick, quick! Angel pulls her suitcase out from under the bed – there are still traces of wedding confetti within – and tap-tap she goes, with sharp little footsteps, from the wardrobe to the bed, from the chest of drawers and back again, not so much packing as retrieving, salvaging. Something out of nothing!

Angel and her predecessor, rescuing each other, since each was incapable of rescuing herself, and rescue always comes, somehow. Or else death.

Tap, tap, back and forth, into the suitcase, out of the house.

The garden gate swings behind her.

Angel, bearing love to a safer place.

1977

Weekend

By seven-thirty they were ready to go. Martha had everything packed into the car and the three children appropriately dressed and in the back seat, complete with educational games and wholewheat biscuits. When everything was ready in the car Martin would switch off the television, come downstairs, lock up the house, front and back, and take the wheel.

Weekend! Only two hours' drive down to the cottage on Friday evenings: three hours' drive back on Sunday nights. The pleasures of greenery and guests in between. They reckoned themselves fortunate, how fortunate!

On Fridays Martha would get home on the bus at six-twelve and prepare tea and sandwiches for the family: then she would strip four beds and put the sheets and quilt covers in the washing machine for Monday: take the country bedding from the airing basket, plus the books and the games, plus the weekend food – acquired at intervals throughout the week, to lessen the load – plus her own folder of work from the office, plus Martin's drawing materials (she was a market researcher in an advertising agency, he a freelance designer) plus hairbrushes, jeans, spare T-shirts, Jolyon's antibiotics (he suffered from sore throats), Jenny's recorder, Jasper's cassette player and so on – ah, the so on! – and would pack them all, skilfully and quickly, into the boot. Very little could be left in the cottage during the week. ('An open invitation to burglars': Martin) Then Martha would run round the house tidying and wiping, doing this and that, finding the cat at one neighbour's and delivering it to another, while the others ate their tea; and would usually, proudly, have everything finished by the time they had eaten their fill. Martin would just catch the BBC2 news, while Martha cleared away the tea table, and the children tossed up for the best positions in the car. 'Martha,' said Martin, tonight, 'you ought to get Mrs Hodder to do more. She takes advantage of you.'

Mrs Hodder came in twice a week to clean. She was over seventy. She charged two pounds an hour. Martha paid her out of her own wages: well, the running of the house was Martha's concern. If Martha chose to go out to work – as was her perfect right, Martin allowed, even though it wasn't the best thing for the children, but that must be Martha's moral responsibility – Martha must surely pay her domestic stand-in. An evident truth, heard loud and clear and frequent in Martin's mouth and Martha's heart.

'I expect you're right,' said Martha. She did not want to argue. Martin had had a long hard week, and now

had to drive. Martha couldn't. Martha's licence had
been suspended four months back for drunken driving.
Everyone agreed that the suspension was unfair: Martha
seldom drank to excess: she was for one thing usually
too busy pouring drinks for other people or washing
other people's glasses to get much inside herself. But
Martin had taken her out to dinner on her birthday, as
was his custom, and exhaustion and excitement mixed
had made her imprudent, and before she knew where
she was, why there she was, in the dock, with a
distorted lamppost to pay for and a new bonnet for
the car and six months' suspension.

So now Martin had to drive her car down to the
cottage, and he was always tired on Fridays, and hot and
sleepy on Sundays, and every rattle and clank and bump
in the engine she felt to be somehow her fault.

Martin had a little sports car for London and work: it
could nip in and out of the traffic nicely: Martha's was
an old estate car, with room for the children, picnic
baskets, bedding, food, games, plants, drink, portable
television and all the things required by the middle
classes for weekends in the country. It lumbered rather
than zipped and made Martin angry. He seldom spoke a
harsh word, but Martha, after the fashion of wives,
could detect his mood from what he did not say rather
than what he did, and from the tilt of his head, and the
way his crinkly, merry eyes seemed crinklier and
merrier still – and of course from the way he addressed
Martha's car.

'Come along, you old banger you! Can't you do
better than that? You're too old, that's your trouble.

Stop complaining. Always complaining, it's only a hill. You're too wide about the hips. You'll never get through there.'

Martha worried about her age, her tendency to complain, and the width of her hips. She took the remarks personally. Was she right to do so? The children noticed nothing: it was just funny lively laughing Daddy being witty about Mummy's car. Mummy, done for drunken driving. Mummy, with the roots of melancholy somewhere deep beneath the bustling, busy, everyday self. Busy: ah so busy!

Martin would only laugh if she said anything about the way he spoke to her car and warn her against paranoia. 'Don't get like your mother, darling.' Martha's mother had, towards the end, thought that people were plotting against her. Martha's mother had led a secluded, suspicious life, and made Martha's childhood a chilly and a lonely time. Life now, by comparison, was wonderful for Martha. People, children, houses, conversations, food, drink, theatres – even, now, a career. Martin standing between her and the hostility of the world – popular, easy, funny Martin, beckoning the rest of the world into earshot.

Ah, she was grateful: little earnest Martha, with her shy ways and her penchant for passing boring exams – how her life had blossomed out! Three children too – Jasper, Jenny and Jolyon – all with Martin's broad brow and open looks, and the confidence born of her love and care, and the work she had put into them since the dawning of their days.

Martin drives. Martha, for once, drowses.

The right food, the right words, the right play. Doctors
for the tonsils: dentists for the molars. Confiscate guns:
censor television: encourage creativity. Paints and paper
to hand: books on the shelves: meetings with teachers.
Music teachers. Dancing lessons. Parties. Friends to tea.
School plays. Open days. Junior orchestra.

Martha is jolted awake. Traffic lights. Martin doesn't
like Martha to sleep while he drives.

Clothes. Oh, clothes! Can't wear this: must wear that.
Dress shops. Piles of clothes in corners: duly washed, but
waiting to be ironed, waiting to be put away.

Get the piles off the floor, into the laundry baskets.
Martin doesn't like a mess.

Creativity arises out of order, not chaos. Five years
off work while the children were small: back to work
with seniority lost. What, did you think something was
for nothing? If you have children, mother, that is your
reward. It lies not in the world.

Have you taken enough food? Always hard to judge.

Food. Oh, food! Shop in the lunch-hour. Lug it all
home. Cook for the freezer on Wednesday evenings
while Martin is at his car-maintenance evening class,
and isn't there to notice you being unrestful. Martin
likes you to sit down in the evenings. Fruit, meat,
vegetables, flour for home-made bread. Well, shop
bread is full of pollutants. Frozen food, even your
own, loses flavour. Martin often remarks on it.

Condiments. Everyone loves mango chutney. But
the expense!

London Airport to the left. Look, look, children!
Concorde? No, idiot, of course it isn't Concorde.

Ah, to be all things to all people: children, husband, employer, friends! It can be done: yes, it can: super woman.

Drink. Home-made wine. Why not? Elderberries grown thick and rich in London: and at least you know what's in it. Store it in high cupboards: lots of room: up and down the step-ladder. Careful! Don't slip. Don't break anything.

No such thing as an accident. Accidents are Freudian slips: they are wilful, bad-tempered things.

Martin can't bear bad temper. Martin likes slim ladies. Diet. Martin rather likes his secretary. Diet. Martin admires slim legs and big bosoms. How to achieve them both? Impossible. But try, oh try, to be what you ought to be, not what you are. Inside and out.

Martin brings back flowers and chocolates: whisks Martha off for holiday weekends. Wonderful! The best husband in the world: look into his crinkly, merry, gentle eyes; see it there. So the mouth slopes away into something of a pout. Never mind. Gaze into the eyes. Love. It must be love. You married him. *You*. Surely *you* deserve true love?

Salisbury Plain. Stonehenge. Look, children, look! Mother, we've seen Stonehenge a hundred times. Go back to sleep.

Cook! Ah cook. People love to come to Martin and Martha's dinners. Work it out in your head in the lunch-hour. If you get in at six-twelve, you can seal the meat while you beat the egg white while you feed the cat while you lay the table while you string the beans while you set out the cheese, goat's cheese, Martin loves goat's cheese, Martha tries to like goat's cheese – oh, bed, sleep, peace, quiet.

Sex! Ah sex. Orgasm, please. Martin requires it. Well, so do you. And you don't want his secretary providing a passion you neglected to develop. Do you? Quick, quick, the cosmic bond. Love. Married love.

Secretary! Probably a vulgar suspicion: nothing more. Probably a fit of paranoics, à la mother, now dead and gone.

At peace.

R.I.P.

Chilly, lonely mother, following her suspicions where they led.

Nearly there, children. Nearly in paradise, nearly at the cottage. Have another biscuit.

Real roses round the door.

Roses. Prune, weed, spray, feed, pick. Avoid thorns. One of Martin's few harsh words.

'Martha, you can't not want roses! What kind of person am I married to? An anti-rose personality?'

Green grass. Oh, God, grass. Grass must be mown. Restful lawns, daisies bobbing, buttercups glowing. Roses and grass and books. Books.

Please, Martin, do we have to have the two hundred books, mostly twenties' first editions, bought at Christie's book sale on one of your afternoons off? Books need dusting.

Roars of laughter from Martin, Jasper, Jenny and Jolyon. Mummy says we shouldn't have the books: books need dusting!

Roses, green grass, books and peace.

Martha woke up with a start when they got to the cottage, and gave a little shriek which made them all laugh. Mummy's waking shriek, they called it.

Then there was the car to unpack and the beds to make up, and the electricity to connect, and the supper to make, and the cobwebs to remove, while Martin made the fire. Then supper – pork chops in sweet and sour sauce ('Pork is such a *dull* meat if you don't cook it properly': Martin), green salad from the garden, or such green salad as the rabbits had left. ('Martha, did you really net them properly? Be honest, now!': Martin) and sauté potatoes. Mash is so stodgy and ordinary, and instant mash unthinkable. The children studied the night sky with the aid of their star map. Wonderful, rewarding children!

Then clear up the supper: set the dough to prove for the bread: Martin already in bed: exhausted by the drive and lighting the fire. ('Martha, we really ought to get the logs stacked properly. Get the children to do it, will you?': Martin) Sweep and tidy: get the TV aerial right. Turn up Jasper's jeans where he has trodden the hem undone. ('He can't go around like *that*, Martha. Not even Jasper': Martin)

Midnight. Good night. Weekend guests arriving in the morning. Seven for lunch and dinner on Saturday. Seven for Sunday breakfast, nine for Sunday lunch. ('Don't fuss, darling. You always make such a fuss': Martin) Oh, God, forgotten the garlic squeezer. That means ten minutes with the back of a spoon and salt. Well, who wants *lumps* of garlic? No one. Not Martin's guests. Martin said so. Sleep.

Colin and Katie. Colin is Martin's oldest friend.
Katie is his new young wife. Janet, Colin's other,
earlier wife, was Martha's friend. Janet was rather like
Martha, quieter and duller than her husband. A nag and
a drag, Martin rather thought, and said, and of course
she'd let herself go, everyone agreed. No one exactly
excused Colin for walking out, but you could see the
temptation.

Katie versus Janet.

Katie was languid, beautiful and elegant. She
drawled when she spoke. Her hands were expres-
sive: her feet were little and female. She had no
children.

Janet plodded round on very flat, rather large feet.
There was something wrong with them. They turned
out slightly when she walked. She had two children.
She was, frankly, boring. But Martha liked her: when
Janet came down to the cottage she would wash up.
Not in the way that most guests washed up – washing
dutifully and setting everything out on the draining
board, but actually drying and putting away too. And
Janet would wash the bath and get the children all sat
down, with chairs for everyone, even the littlest, and
keep them quiet and satisfied so the grown-ups – well,
the men – could get on with their conversation and
their jokes and their love of country weekends, while
Janet stared into space, as if grateful for the rest, quite
happy.

Janet would garden, too. Weed the strawberries,
while the men went for their walk; her great feet
standing firm and square and sometimes crushing a

plant or so, but never mind, oh never mind. Lovely Janet; who understood.

Now Janet was gone and here was Katie.

Katie talked with the men and went for walks with the men, and moved her ashtray rather impatiently when Martha tried to clear the drinks round it.

Dishes were boring, Katie implied by her manner, and domesticity was boring, and anyone who bothered with that kind of thing was a fool. Like Martha. Ash should be allowed to stay where it was, even if it was in the butter, and conversations should never be interrupted.

Knock, knock. Katie and Colin arrived at one-fifteen on Saturday morning, just after Martha had got to bed. 'You don't mind? It was the moonlight. We couldn't resist it. You should have seen Stonehenge! We didn't disturb you? Such early birds!'

Martha rustled up a quick meal of omelettes. Saturday nights' eggs. ('Martha makes a lovely omelette': Martin) ('Honey, make one of your mushroom omelettes: cook the mushrooms separately, remember, with lemon. Otherwise the water from the mushrooms gets into the egg, and spoils everything.') Sunday supper mushrooms. But ungracious to say anything.

Martin had revived wonderfully at the sight of Colin and Katie. He brought out the whisky bottle. Glasses. Ice. Jug for water. Wait. Wash up another sinkful, when they're finished. 2 a.m.

'Don't do it tonight, darling.'

'It'll only take a sec.' Bright smile, not a hint of self-pity. Self-pity can spoil everyone's weekend.

Martha knows that if breakfast for seven is to be manageable the sink must be cleared of dishes. A tricky meal, breakfast. Especially if bacon, eggs, and tomatoes must all be cooked in separate pans. ('Separate pans mean separate flavours!': Martin)

She is running around in her nightie. Now if that had been Katie – but there's something so *practical* about Martha. Reassuring, mind; but the skimpy nightie and the broad rump and the thirty-eight years are all rather embarrassing. Martha can see it in Colin and Katie's eyes. Martin's too. Martha wishes she did not see so much in other people's eyes. Her mother did, too. Dear, dead mother. Did I misjudge you?

This was the second weekend Katie had been down with Colin but without Janet. Colin was a photographer: Katie had been his accessoriser. First Colin and Janet: then Colin, Janet and Katie: now Colin and Katie!

Katie weeded with rubber gloves on and pulled out pansies in mistake for weeds and laughed and laughed along with everyone when her mistake was pointed out to her, but the pansies died. Well, Colin had become with the years fairly rich and fairly famous, and what does a fairly rich and famous man want with a wife like Janet when Katie is at hand?

On the first of the Colin/Janet/Katie weekends Katie had appeared out of the bathroom. 'I say,' said Katie, holding out a damp towel with evident distaste, 'I can only find this. No hope of a dry one?' And Martha had run to fetch a dry towel and amazingly found one, and handed it to Katie who flashed her a brilliant smile and said, 'I can't bear damp towels. Anything in the world but damp towels,' as if speaking to a servant in a time of shortage of staff, and took all the water so there was none left for Martha to wash up.

The trouble, of course, was drying anything at all in the cottage. There were no facilities for doing so, and Martin had a horror of clothes lines which might spoil the view. He toiled and moiled all week in the city simply to get a country view at the weekend. Ridiculous to spoil it by draping it with wet towels! But now Martha had bought more towels, so perhaps everyone could be satisfied. She would take nine damp towels back on Sunday evenings in a plastic bag and see to them in London.

On this Saturday morning, straight after breakfast, Katie went out to the car – she and Colin had a new Lamborghini; hard to imagine Katie in anything duller – and came back waving a new Yves St Laurent towel. 'See! I brought my own, darlings.'

They'd brought nothing else. No fruit, no meat, no vegetables, not even bread, certainly not a box of chocolates. They'd gone off to bed with alacrity, the night before, and the spare room rocked and heaved: well, who'd want to do washing-up when you could do that, but what about the children? Would they get confused? First Colin and Janet, now Colin and Katie?

Martha murmured something of her thoughts to Martin, who looked quite shocked. 'Colin's my best friend. I don't expect him to bring anything,' and Martha felt mean. 'And good heavens, you can't protect the kids from sex for ever; don't be so prudish,' so that Martha felt stupid as well. Mean, complaining, and stupid.

Janet had rung Martha during the week. The house had been sold over her head, and she and the children had been moved into a small flat. Katie was trying to persuade Colin to cut down on her allowance, Janet said.

'It does one no good to be materialistic,' Katie confided. 'I have nothing. No home, no family, no ties, no possessions. Look at me! Only me and a suitcase of clothes.' But Katie seemed highly satisfied with the me, and the clothes were stupendous. Katie drank a great deal and became funny. Everyone laughed, including Martha. Katie had been married twice. Martha marvelled at how someone could arrive in their mid-thirties with nothing at all to their name, neither husband, nor children, nor property and not mind.

Mind you, Martha could see the power of such helplessness. If Colin was all Katie had in the world, how could Colin abandon her? And to what? Where would she go? How would she live? Oh, clever Katie.

'My teacup's dirty,' said Katie, and Martha ran to clean it, apologising, and Martin raised his eyebrows, at Martha, not Katie.

'I wish *you'd* wear scent,' said Martin to Martha, reproachfully. Katie wore lots. Martha never seemed to have time to put any on, though Martin bought her bottle after bottle. Martha leapt out of bed each morning to meet some emergency – miaowing cat, coughing child, faulty alarm clock, postman's knock –

when was Martha to put on scent? It annoyed Martin all the same. She ought to do more to charm him.

Colin looked handsome and harrowed and younger than Martin, though they were much the same age. 'Youth's catching,' said Martin in bed that night. 'It's since he found Katie.' Found, like some treasure. Discovered; something exciting and wonderful, in the dreary world of established spouses.

On Saturday morning Jasper trod on a piece of wood ('Martha, why isn't he wearing shoes? It's too bad': Martin) and Martha took him into the hospital to have a nasty splinter removed. She left the cottage at ten and arrived back at one, and they were still sitting in the sun, drinking, empty bottles glinting in the long grass. The grass hadn't been cut. Don't forget the bottles. Broken glass means more mornings at the hospital. Oh, don't fuss. Enjoy yourself. Like other people. Try.

But no potatoes peeled, no breakfast cleared, nothing. Cigarette ends still amongst old toast, bacon rind and marmalade. 'You could have done the potatoes,' Martha burst out. Oh, bad temper! Prime sin. They looked at her in amazement and dislike. Martin too.

'Goodness,' said Katie. 'Are we doing the whole Sunday lunch bit on Saturday? Potatoes? Ages since I've eaten potatoes. Wonderful!'

'The children expect it,' said Martha.

So they did. Saturday and Sunday lunch shone like reassuring beacons in their lives. Saturday lunch: family lunch: fish and chips. ('So much better cooked at home than bought': Martin) Sunday. Usually roast beef, potatoes, peas, apple pie. Oh, of course. Yorkshire pudding. Always a problem with oven temperatures. When the beef's going slowly, the Yorkshire should be going fast. How to achieve that? Like big bosom and little hips.

'Just relax,' said Martin. 'I'll cook dinner, all in good time. Splinters always work their own way out: no need to have taken him to hospital. Let life drift over you, my love. Flow with the waves, that's the way.'

And Martin flashed Martha a distant, spiritual smile. His hand lay on Katie's slim brown arm, with its many gold bands.

'Anyway, you do too much for the children,' said Martin. 'It isn't good for them. Have a drink.'

So Martha perched uneasily on the step and had a glass of cider, and wondered how, if lunch was going to be late, she would get cleared up and the meat out of the marinade for the rather formal dinner that would be expected that evening. The marinaded lamb ought to cook for at least four hours in a low oven; and the cottage oven was very small, and you couldn't use that and the grill at the same time and Martin liked his fish grilled, not fried. Less cholesterol.

She didn't say as much. Domestic details like this were very boring, and any mild complaint was registered by Martin as a scene. And to make a scene was so ungrateful.

This was the life. Well, wasn't it? Smart friends in large cars and country living and drinks before lunch and roses and bird song – 'Don't drink *too* much,' said Martin, and told them about Martha's suspended driving licence.

The children were hungry so Martha opened them a can of beans and sausages and heated that up. ('Martha, do they have to eat that crap? Can't they wait?': Martin)

Katie was hungry: she said so, to keep the children in face. She was lovely with children – most children. She did not particularly like Colin and Janet's children. She said so, and he accepted it. He only saw them once a month now, not once a week.

'Let me make lunch,' Katie said to Martha. 'You do so much, poor thing!'

And she pulled out of the fridge all the things Martha had put away for the next day's picnic lunch party – Camembert cheese and salad and salami and made a wonderful tomato salad in two minutes and opened the white wine – 'not very cold, darling. Shouldn't it be chilling?' – and had it all on the table in five amazing competent minutes. 'That's all we need, darling,' said Martin. 'You are funny with your fish-and-chip Saturdays! What could be nicer than this? Or simpler?'

Nothing, except there was Sunday's buffet lunch for nine gone, in place of Saturday's fish for six, and would the fish stretch? No. Katie had had quite a lot to drink. She pecked Martha on the forehead. 'Funny little Martha,' she said. 'She reminds me of Janet. I really do like Janet.' Colin did not want to be reminded of Janet, and said so. 'Darling, Janet's a fact of life,' said Katie. 'If you'd only think about her more, you might manage to pay her less.' And she yawned and stretched her lean, childless body and smiled at Colin with her inviting, naughty little girl eyes, and Martin watched her in admiration.

Martha got up and left them and took a paint pot and put a coat of white gloss on the bathroom wall. The white surface pleased her. She was good at painting. She produced a smooth, even surface. Her legs throbbed. She feared she might be getting varicose veins.

Outside in the garden the children played badminton. They were bad-tempered, but relieved to be able to look up and see their mother working, as usual: making their lives for ever better and nicer: organising, planning, thinking ahead, side-stepping disaster, making preparations, like a mother hen, fussing and irritating: part of the natural boring scenery of the world.

On Saturday night Katie went to bed early: she rose from her chair and stretched and yawned and poked her head into the kitchen where Martha was washing saucepans.

Colin had cleared the table and Katie had folded the napkins into pretty creases, while Martin blew at the fire, to make it bright. 'Good night,' said Katie.

Katie appeared three minutes later, reproachfully holding out her Yves St Laurent towel, sopping wet. 'Oh dear,' cried Martha. 'Jenny must have washed her hair!' And Martha was obliged to rout Jenny out of bed to rebuke her, publicly, if only to demonstrate that she knew what was right and proper. That meant Jenny would sulk all weekend, and that meant a treat or an outing mid-week, or else by the following week she'd be having an asthma attack.

'You fuss the children too much,' said Martin. 'That's why Jenny has asthma.' Jenny was pleasant enough to look at, but not stunning. Perhaps she was a disappointment to her father? Martin would never say so, but Martha feared he thought so.

An egg and an orange each child, each day. Then nothing too bad would go wrong. And it hadn't. The asthma was very mild. A calm, tranquil environment, the doctor said. Ah, smile, Martha smile. Domestic happiness depends on you. 21 × 52 oranges a year. Each one to be purchased, carried, peeled and washed up after. And what about potatoes. 12 × 52 pounds a year? Martin liked his potatoes carefully peeled. He couldn't bear to find little cores of black in the mouthful. ('Well, it isn't very nice, is it?': Martin)

Martha dreamt she was eating coal, by handfuls, and liking it.

Saturday night. Martin made love to Martha three times. Three times? How virile he was, and clearly turned on by the sounds from the spare room. Martin said he loved her. Martin always did. He was a courteous lover; he knew the importance of fore-play. So did Martha. Three times.

Ah, sleep. Jolyon had a nightmare. Jenny was woken by a moth. Martin slept through everything. Martha pottered about the house in the night. There was a moon. She sat at the window and stared out into the summer night for five minutes, and was at peace, and then went back to bed because she ought to be fresh for the morning.

But she wasn't. She slept late. The others went out for a walk. They'd left a note, a considerate note: 'Didn't wake you. You looked tired. Had a cold breakfast so as not to make too much mess. Leave everything 'til we get back.' But it was ten o'clock, and guests were coming at noon, so she cleared away the bread, the butter, the crumbs, the smears, the jam, the spoons, the spilt sugar, the cereal, the milk (sour by now) and the dirty plates, and swept the floors, and tidied up quickly, and grabbed a cup of coffee, and prepared to make a rice and fish dish, and a chocolate mousse and sat down in the middle to eat a lot of bread and jam herself. Broad hips. She remembered the office work in her file and knew she wouldn't be able to do it. Martin anyway thought it was ridiculous for her to bring work back at the weekends. 'It's your holiday,' he'd say. 'Why should they impose?' Martha loved her work. She didn't have to smile at it. She just did it.

Katie came back upset and crying. She sat in the kitchen while Martha worked and drank glass after glass of gin and bitter lemon. Katie liked ice and lemon in gin. Martha paid for all the drink out of her wages. It was part of the deal between her and Martin – the contract by which she went out to work. All things to cheer the spirit, otherwise depressed by a working wife and mother, were to be paid for by Martha. Drink, holidays, petrol, outings, puddings, electricity, heating: it was quite a joke between them. It didn't really make any difference: it was their joint money, after all. Amazing how Martha's wages were creeping up, almost to the level of Martin's. One day they would overtake. Then what?

Work, honestly, was a piece of cake.

Anyway, poor Katie was crying. Colin, she'd discovered, kept a photograph of Janet and the children in his wallet. 'He's not free of her. He pretends he is, but he isn't. She has him by a stranglehold. It's the kids. His bloody kids. Moaning Mary and that little creep Joanna. It's all he thinks about. I'm nobody.'

But Katie didn't believe it. She knew she was somebody all right. Colin came in, in a fury. He took out the photograph and set fire to it, bitterly, with a match. Up in smoke they went. Mary and Joanna and Janet. The ashes fell on the floor. (Martha swept them up when Colin and Katie had gone. It hardly seemed polite to do so when they were still there.) 'Go back to her,' Katie said. 'Go back to her. I don't care. Honestly, I'd rather be on my own. You're a nice old-fashioned thing. Run along then. Do your thing, I'll do mine. Who cares?'

'Christ, Katie, the fuss! She only just happens to be in the photograph. She's not there on purpose to annoy. And I do feel bad about her. She's been having a hard time.'

'And haven't you, Colin? She twists a pretty knife, I can tell you. Don't you have rights too? Not to mention me. Is a little loyalty too much to expect?'

They were reconciled before lunch, up in the spare room. Harry and Beryl Elder arrived at twelve-thirty. Harry didn't like to hurry on Sundays; Beryl was flustered with apologies for their lateness. They'd brought artichokes from their garden. 'Wonderful,' cried Martin. 'Fruits of the earth? Let's have a wonderful soup! Don't fret, Martha. I'll do it.'

'Don't fret.' Martha clearly hadn't been smiling enough. She was in danger, Martin implied, of ruining everyone's weekend. There was an emergency in the garden very shortly – an elm tree which had probably got Dutch elm disease – and Martha finished the artichokes. The lid flew off the blender and there was artichoke purée everywhere. 'Let's have lunch outside,' said Colin. 'Less work for Martha.'

Martin frowned at Martha: he thought the appearance of martyrdom in the face of guests to be an unforgivable offence.

Everyone happily joined in taking the furniture out, but it was Martha's experience that nobody ever helped to bring it in again. Jolyon was stung by a wasp. Jasper sneezed and sneezed from hay fever and couldn't find the tissues and he wouldn't use loo paper. ('Surely you remembered the tissues, darling?': Martin)

Beryl Elder was nice. 'Wonderful to eat out,' she said, fetching the cream for her pudding, while Martha fished a fly from the liquefying Brie ('You shouldn't have bought it so ripe, Martha': Martin) – 'except it's just some other woman has to do it. But at least it isn't *me*.' Beryl worked too, as a secretary, to send the boys to boarding school, where she'd rather they weren't. But her husband was from a rather grand family, and she'd been only a typist when he married her, so her life was a mass of amends, one way or another. Harry had lately opted out of the stockbroking rat race and become an artist, choosing integrity rather than money, but that choice was his alone and couldn't of course be inflicted on the boys.

Katie found the fish and rice dish rather strange, toyed at it with her fork, and talked about Italian restaurants she knew. Martin lay back soaking in the sun: crying, 'Oh, this is the life.' He made coffee, nobly, and the lid flew off the grinder and there were coffee beans all over the kitchen especially in amongst the row of cookery books which Martin gave Martha Christmas by Christmas. At least they didn't have to be brought back every weekend. ('The burglars won't have the sense to steal those': Martin)

Beryl fell asleep and Katie watched her, quizzically. Beryl's mouth was open and she had a lot of fillings, and her ankles were thick and her waist was going, and she didn't look after herself. 'I love women,' sighed Katie. 'They look so wonderful asleep. I wish I could be an earth mother.'

Beryl woke with a start and nagged her husband into going home, which he clearly didn't want to do, so didn't. Beryl thought she had to get back because his mother was coming round later. Nonsense! Then Beryl tried to stop Harry drinking more home-made wine and was laughed at by everyone. He was driving, Beryl couldn't, and he did have a nasty scar on his temple from a previous road accident. Never mind.

'She does come on strong, poor soul,' laughed Katie when they'd finally gone. 'I'm never going to get married,' – and Colin looked at her yearningly because he wanted to marry her more than anything in the world, and Martha cleared the coffee cups.

'Oh don't *do* that,' said Katie, 'do just sit *down*, Martha, you make us all feel bad,' and Martin glared at

Martha who sat down and Jenny called out for her and
Martha went upstairs and Jenny had started her first
period and Martha cried and cried and knew she must
stop because this must be a joyous occasion for Jenny or
her whole future would be blighted, but for once,
Martha couldn't.

Her daughter Jenny: wife, mother, friend.

1978

Horrors of the Road

Miss Jacobs, I don't believe in psychotherapy. I really do think it's a lot of nonsense. Now it's taken me considerable nerve to say that – I'm a rather mild person and hate to be thought rude. I just wouldn't want to be here under false pretences: it wouldn't be fair to you, would it?

But Piers wants me to come and see you, so of course I will. He's waiting outside in your pretty drawing room: I said he should go, and come back when the session was up: that I'd be perfectly all right but he likes to be at hand in case anything happens. Just sometimes I do fall forward, out of my chair – so far I haven't hurt myself. Once it was face-first into a feather sofa; the second was trickier – I was with Martin – he's my little grandchild, you know, David's boy, the only one so far – at the sandpit in the park and I just pitched forward into the sand. Someone sent for an ambulance but it wasn't really necessary – I was perfectly all right, instantly. Well, except for this one big permanent fact that my legs don't work.

I'm a great mystery to the doctors. Piers has taken me everywhere – Paris, New York, Tokyo – but the verdict seems to be the same: it's all in my head. It is a hysterical paralysis. I find this humiliating: as if I'd done it on purpose just to be a nuisance. I'm the last person in the world to be a nuisance!

Did you see Piers? Isn't he handsome? He's in his mid-fifties, you know, but so good-looking. Of course he has an amazing brain – well, the whole world knows that – and I think that helps to keep people looking young. I have a degree in Economics myself – unusual for a housewife of my age – but of course I stayed home to devote myself to Piers and the children. I think, on the whole, women should do that. Don't you? Why don't you answer my questions? Isn't that what you're supposed to do? Explain me to myself? No?

I must explain myself to myself! Oh.

Behind every great man stands a woman. I believe that. Piers is a Nobel Prize winner. Would he have done it without me? I expect so. He just wouldn't have had me, would he, or the four children? They're all doing very well. Piers was away quite a lot when the children were young – he's a particle physicist, as I'm sure you know. He had to be away. They don't keep cyclotrons in suitably domestic places, and the money had to be earned somehow. But we all always had these holidays together, in France. How we loved France. How well we knew it. Piers would drive; I'd navigate; the four children piled in the back! Of course these days we fly. There's just Piers and me. It's glamorous and exciting, and people know who he is so the service is good. Waiters don't mind so much . . . Mind what? . . . I thought you weren't supposed to ask questions. I was talking about holidays, in the past, long ago. Well, not so long ago. We went on till the youngest was fifteen; Brutus that is, and he's only twenty now. Can it be only five years?

I miss those summer dockside scenes: the cars lined up at dusk or dawn waiting for the ferry home: sunburned families, careless and exhausted after weeks in the sun. By careless I don't mean without care – just without caring any more. They'll sleep all night in their cars to be first in the queue for the ferry, and not worry about it; on the journey out they'd have gone berserk. Brown faces and brittle blonde hair and grubby children; and the roof-racks with the tents and the water cans and the boxes of wine and strings of garlic. Volvos and Cortinas and Volkswagen vans.

Of course our cars never looked smart: we even started out once with a new one, but by the time we came back it was dented and bumped and battered. French drivers are so dreadful, aren't they; and their road signs are impossible.

How did the paralysis start? It was completely unexpected. There were no warning signs – no numbness, no dizziness, nothing like that. It was our thirtieth wedding anniversary. To celebrate we were going to do a tour of France in Piers' new MG. It can do 110 mph, you know, but Piers doesn't often go at more than fifty-five – that's the speed limit in the States, you know, and he says they know what they're doing – it's the best speed for maximum safety – but he likes to have cars that can go fast. To get out of trouble in an emergency, Piers says. We were going on the

Weymouth/Cherbourg route – I'm usually happier with Dover/Calais – the sea journey's shorter for one thing, and somehow the longer the journey through England the more likely Piers is to forget to drive on the right once we're in France. I've noticed it. But I don't argue about things like that. Piers knows what he's doing – I never backseat drive. I'm his wife, he's my husband. We love each other.

So we were setting out for Weymouth, the bags were packed, the individual route maps from the AA in the glove compartment – they'd arrived on time, for once. (I'd taken a Valium in good time – my heart tends to beat rather fast, almost to the point of palpitations, when I'm navigating.) I was wearing a practical non-crease dress – you know what long journeys are like – you always end up a little stained. Piers loves melons and likes me to feed him wedges as we drive along – and you know how ripe a ripe French melon can be. Piers will spend hours choosing one from a market stall. He'll test every single one on display – you know, sniffing and pressing the ends for just the right degree of tenderness – until he's found one that's absolutely perfect. Sometimes, before he's satisfied, he'll go through the fruit boxes at the back of the stall as well. The French like you to be particular, Piers says. They'll despise you if you accept just anything. And then, of course, if the melon's not to go over the top, they have to be eaten quite quickly – in the car as often as not . . .

Anyway, as I was saying, I was about to step into the car when my legs just kind of folded and I sank down on to the pavement, and that was six months ago, and I haven't walked since. No, no palpitations since either. I can't remember if I had palpitations before I was married – I've been married for ever!

And there was no holiday. Just me paralysed. No tour of France. Beautiful France. I adore the Loire and the châteaux, don't you? The children loved the West Coast: those stretches of piny woods and the long, long beaches and the great Atlantic rollers – but after the middle of August the winds change and everything gets dusty and somehow grizzly. When the children were small we camped, but every year the sites got more formal and more crowded and more full of *frites* and Piers didn't like that. He enjoyed what he called 'wilderness camping'. In the camping guides which describe the sites there's always an area section – that is, the area allowed for each tent. Point five of a hectare is crowded: two hectares perfectly possible. Piers liked ten hectares, which meant a hillside somewhere and no television room for the children or *frites* stall – and that meant more work for me, not that I grudged it: a change of venue for cooking – such lovely portable calor gas stoves we had: you could do a three-course meal on just two burners if you were clever, if the wind wasn't too high – is as good as a rest from cooking. It was just that the children preferred the crowded sites, and I did sometimes think they were better for the children's French. An English sparrow and a French sparrow sing pretty much the same song. But there you are, Piers loved the wilderness. He'd always measure the actual hectarage available for our tent, and if it didn't coincide with what was in the book would take it up with the relevant authorities. I remember it once ending up with people having to move their tents at ten in the evening to make proper room for ours – we'd driven three hundred miles that day and Brutus was only two. That wasn't Piers' fault: it was the camp proprietor's. Piers merely knocked him up to point out that our site wasn't the dimension it ought to be, and he over-reacted quite dreadfully. I was glad to get away from that site in the morning, I can tell you. It really wasn't Piers' fault; just one of those things. I'm glad it was only a stop-over. The other campers just watched us go, in complete silence. It was weird. And Fanny cried all the way to Poitiers.

Such a tearful little thing, Fanny. Piers liked to have a picnic lunch at about three o'clock – the French roads clear at mid-day while everyone goes off to gorge themselves on lunch, so you can make really good time wherever you're going. Sometimes I did wonder where it was we *were* going to, or *why* we had to make such time, but on the other hand those wonderful white empty B roads, poplar-lined, at a steady 55 mph . . . anyway, we'd buy our lunch at mid-day – wine and pâté and long French bread and orangina for the children, and then at three start looking for a nice place to picnic. Nothing's harder! If the place is right, the traffic's wrong. Someone's on your tail hooting – how those French drivers do hoot – they can see the GB plates – they know it means the driver's bound to forget and go round roundabouts the wrong way – and before you know it the ideal site is passed. The ideal site has a view, no snakes, some sun and some shade, and I like to feel the car's right off the road – especially if it's a Route Nationale – though Piers doesn't worry too much. Once actually some idiot did drive right into it – he didn't brake in time – but as Piers had left our car in gear, and not put on the handbrake or anything silly, it just shot forward and not much damage was done.

How is it that other cars always look so smooth and somehow new? I suppose their owners must just keep them in garages all the time having the bumps knocked out and re-sprays – well, fools and their money are often parted, as Piers keeps saying.

What was I talking about? Stopping for lunch. Sometimes it would be four thirty before we found somewhere really nice, and by four you could always rely on Fanny to start crying. I'd give her water from the Pschitt bottle – how the children giggled – Pschitt – every year a ritual, lovely giggle – and break off bread from the loaf for her, but still she grizzled: and Daddy would stop and start and stare over hedges and go a little way down lanes and find them impossible and back out on to the main road, and the children would fall silent, except for Fanny. Aren't French drivers rude? Had you noticed? I'd look sideways at a passing car and the driver would be staring at us, screwing his thumb into his head, or pretending to slit his throat with his finger – and always these honks and hoots, and once someone pulled in and forced us to stop and tried to drag poor Piers out of the car, goodness knows why. Just general Gallic over-excitement, I suppose. Piers is a wonderfully safe driver. I do think he sometimes

inconveniences other cars the way he stops at inter-
sections – you know how muddling their road signs
are, especially on city ring roads, and how they seem to
be telling you to go right or left when actually they
mean straight on. And Piers is a scientist – he likes to be
sure he's doing the right thing. I have the maps; I do my
best: I memorise whole areas of the country, so I will
know when passing through, say, Limoges, on the way
from Périgueux to Issoudun, and have to make lightning decisions – Piers seems to speed up in towns. No!
Not the Tulle road, not the Clermont road, not the
Montluçon but the Châteauroux road. Only the
Châteauroux road isn't marked! Help! What's its
number? Dear God, it's the N20! We'll die! The
N147 to Bellac then, and cut through on the B roads
to Argenton, La Châtre . . . So look for the Poitiers
sign. Bellac's on the road to Poitiers –

So he stops, if he's not convinced I'm right, and takes
the map himself and studies it before going on. Which
meant, in later years, finding his magnifying glass. He
hates spectacles! And you know what those overhead
traffic lights are like in small country towns, impossible
to see, so no one takes any notice of them! Goodness
knows how French drivers survive at all. We had one
or two nasty misses through no fault of our own every
holiday; I did in the end feel happier if I took Valium.
But I never liked Piers to know I was taking it – it
seemed a kind of statement of lack of faith – which is
simply untrue. Look at the way he carried me in,
cradled me in his arms, laid me on this sofa! I trust him
implicitly. I am his wife. He is my husband.

What was I saying? Fanny grizzling. She took off to New Zealand as soon as she'd finished her college course. A long way away. Almost as far as she could get, I find myself saying, I don't know why. I know she loves us and we certainly love her. She writes frequently. David's a racing car driver. Piers and I are very upset about this. Such a dangerous occupation. Those cars get up to 200 mph – and Piers did so hate speed. Angela's doing psychiatric nursing. They say she has a real gift for it.

I remember once I said to Piers – we were on the ring road round Angers – turn left here, meaning the T-junction we were approaching – but he swung straight left across the other carriageway, spying a little side road there – empty because all the traffic was round the corner, held up by the lights, ready to surge forward. He realised what he'd done, and stopped, leaving us broadside across the main road. 'Reverse!' I shrieked, breaking my rule about no backseat driving, and he did, and we were just out of the way when the expected wall of traffic bore down. 'You should have said second left,' he said, 'that was very nearly a multiple pile-up!' You can't be too careful in France. They're mad drivers, as everyone knows. And with the children in the car too –

But it was all such fun. Piers always knew how to get the best out of waiters and chefs. He'd go right through the menu with the waiter, asking him to explain each dish. If the waiter couldn't do it – and it's amazing how many waiters can't – he would send for the chef and ask him. It did get a little embarrassing sometimes, if the restaurant was very busy, but as Piers said, the French understand food and really appreciate it if you do too. I can make up my mind in a flash what I want to eat: Piers takes ages. As I say, he hates to get things wrong. We'd usually be last to leave any restaurant we ate in, but Piers doesn't believe in hurrying. As he says, a) it's bad for the digestion and b) they don't mind: they're glad to see us appreciating what they have to offer. So many people don't. French waiters are such a rude breed, don't you think? They always seem to have kind of glassy eyes. Goodness knows what they're like if you're *not* appreciating what they have to offer!

And then wine. Piers believes in sending wine back as well as food. Standards have to be maintained. He doesn't believe in serving red wines chilled in the modern fashion, no matter how new they are. And that a bottle of wine under eight francs is as worth discussing as one at thirty francs. He's always very polite: just sends for the wine waiter to discuss the matter, but of course he doesn't speak French, so difficulties sometimes arise. Acrimony almost. And this kind of funny silence while we leave.

And always when we paid the bill before leaving our hotel, Piers would check and re-check every item. He's got rather short-sighted over the years: he has to use a magnifying glass. The children and I would sit waiting in the car for up to an hour while they discussed the cost of hot water and what a reasonable profit was, and why it being a fête holiday should make a difference. I do sometimes think, I admit, that Piers has a love/hate relationship with France. He loves the country; he

won't go holidaying in Italy or Spain, only France –
and yet, you know, those *Dégustation-Libres* that have
sprung up all over the place – 'free disgustings', as the
children call them – where you taste the wine before
choosing? Piers goes in, tastes everything, and if he likes
nothing – which is quite often – buys nothing. That,
after all, is what they are offering. *Free* wine-tasting. He
likes me to go in with him, to taste with him, so that we
can compare notes, and I watch the enthusiasm dying
in the proprietor's eyes, as he is asked to fetch first this,
then that, then the other down from the top shelf, and
Piers sips and raises his eyebrows and shakes his head,
and then hostility dawns in the shopkeeper's eye, and
then boredom, and then I almost think something
which borders on derision – and I must tell you, Miss
Jacobs, I don't like it, and in the end, whenever we
passed a *Dégustation-Libre* and I saw the glint in his eye,
and his foot went on the brake – he never looked in his
mirror – there was no point, since it was always adjusted
to show the car roof – I'd take another Valium – because
I think otherwise I would scream, I couldn't help myself.
It wasn't that I didn't love and trust and admire Piers, it
was the look in the French eye –

Why don't I scream? What are you after? Abreac-
tion? I know the terms – my daughter Angela's a
psychiatric nurse, as I told you, and doing very well.
You think I was finally traumatised at the last *Dégusta-
tion*? And that's why I can't walk? You'd like to believe
that, wouldn't you? I expect you're a feminist – I notice
you're wearing a trouser suit – and like to think
everything in this world is the man's fault. You want

me to scream out tension and rage and terror and horror? I won't! I tell you, France is a joyous place and we all loved those holidays and had some wonderful meals and some knock-out wines, thanks to Piers, and as for his driving, we're all alive, aren't we? Piers, me, David, Angela, Fanny, Brutus. All alive! That must prove something. It's just I don't seem able to walk, and if you would be so kind as to call Piers, he will shift me from your sofa to the chair and wheel me home. Talking will get us nowhere. I do love my husband.

1984

In the Great War

Enid's mother Patty didn't stand a chance. That was in
the Great War, in the fifties, when women were at war
with women. Victory meant a soft bed and an easy life:
defeat meant loneliness and the humiliation of the
spinster. These days, of course, women have declared
themselves allies, and united in a new war, a cold war,
against the common enemy, man. But then, in the
Great War, things were very different. And Patty didn't
stand a chance against Helene. She was, for one thing,
badly equipped for battle. Her legs were thick and
practical, her breasts floppy, and her features, though
pleasant enough, lacked erotic impact. Her blue eyes
were watery and her hair frizzy and cut brusquely for
easy washing and combing. 'I can't stand all this dolling
up,' she'd say. 'What's the point?'

Patty cooked with margarine because it was cheaper
than butter and her white sauces were always lumpy.
She wouldn't keep pot plants, or souvenirs, or even a
cat. What was the point?

She didn't like sex and, though she never refused her
husband Arthur, she washed so carefully before and

after, she made him feel he must have been really rather dirty.

Patty, in other words, was what she was, and saw no point in pretending to be anything else. Or in cooking with mushrooms or holidaying abroad or buying a new pair of shoes for Enid, her only child, when she had a perfectly good pair already, or going with her husband to the pub. And, indeed, there very often was no point in these things, except surely life must be more than something just to be practically and sensibly *got through*?

Enid thought so. Enid thought she'd do better than her mother in the Great War. Enid buffed her pre-pubertal nails and arranged wild flowers in jam jars and put them on the kitchen table. Perhaps she could see what was coming!

For all Patty's good qualities – cleanliness, honesty, thrift, reliability, kindness, sobriety, and so on – did her no good whatsoever when Helene came along. Or so Enid observed. Patty was asleep on duty, and there all of a sudden was Helene, the enemy at the gate, with her slim legs and her bedroom eyes, enticing Arthur away. 'But what does she *see* in Arthur?' asked Patty, dumb-founded. What you don't! the ten-year-old Enid thought, but did not say.

In fact, the Second World Male War, from 1939 to 1945, which men had waged among themselves in the name of Democracy, Freedom, Racial Supremacy and so forth, to the great detriment of women and children everywhere, had sharpened the savagery of the Female War. There just weren't enough men to go around. In ordinary times Helene would have gone into battle for some unmarried professional man – accountant or executive – but having lost country, home, family and friends in the ruins of Berlin now laid claim to Arthur, Patty's husband, a railway engineer in the north of England, who painted portraits as a hobby. The battle she fought for him was short and sharp. She shaved her shapely legs and flashed her liquid eyes.

'She's no better than a whore,' said Patty. 'Shaving her legs!' If God put hairs on your legs, thought Patty, then a woman's duty, and her husband's, too, is to put up with them.

Helene thought otherwise. And in her eyes Arthur saw the promise of secret bliss, the complicity of abandon, and all the charm of sin: the pink of her rosy nipples suffused the new world she offered him. And so, without much difficulty Helene persuaded Arthur to leave Patty and Enid, give up his job, paint pictures for a living and think the world well lost for love.

By some wonderful fluke – wonderful, that is, for Arthur and Helene, if infuriating for Patty – Arthur's paintings were an outstanding commercial success. They became the worst bestselling paintings of the sixties, and Arthur, safely divorced from Patty, lived happily ever after with Helene, painting the occasional painting of wide-eyed deer, and sipping champagne by the side of swimming pools. 'Nasty acidy stuff, champagne,' said Patty.

Enid – Patty and Arthur's daughter – never really forgave her mother for losing the war. As if poor Patty didn't have enough to put up with already, without being blamed by her daughter for something she could hardly help! But that's the way these things go – life is the opposite of fair. It stuns you one moment and trips your feet from under you the next, and then jumps up and down on you, pound, pound, pound for good measure.

You should have seen Enid, when she was twelve, twisting the knife in her mother's wounds, poking about among the lumps of the cauliflower cheese, saying: 'Do we *have* to eat this? No wonder Dad left home!' 'Eat it up, it's good for you,' her mother would reply. 'If you want something fancy go and live with your stepmother.'

And, indeed, Enid had been asked, but Enid never went. Enid would twist a knife but not deliver a mortal wound, not to her mother. Instead she took up the armoury her mother never wore, breathed on it, burnished it, sharpened its cutting edges, prepared for war herself. Long after the war was over, Enid was still fighting. She was like some mad Aussie soldier hiding out in the Malayan jungle, still looking for a foe that had years since thrown away its grenades and taken to TV assembly instead.

At sixteen Enid scanned the fashion pages and read hints on make-up and how to be an interesting person; she went weekly to the theatre and art galleries and classical music concerts and exercised every day, and not until she was eighteen did she feel properly prepared to step into the battlefield. She was intelligent, and thought it sensible enough to go to university, although she chose English literature as the subject least likely to put men off.

'Nothing puts a man off like a clever woman,' said Helene when Enid visited. Now warriors in the Great War thought nothing of swapping secrets. Intelligence services of warring countries, hand in glove, glove in hand! It's always been so. Just as there's always been trade with enemy nations, unofficially if not officially. Helene lisped out quite a few secrets to Enid: her accent tinged with all the poise and decadence of a vanished Europe. 'My foreign wife!' Arthur would say, proudly in his honest, northern, jovial, middle-aged voice. Arthur was the J. B. Priestley of the art world – good in spite of himself.

Oh, Patty had lost a lovely prize, Enid knew it! Her beloved father! What a victory Patty's could have been – and yet she chose defeat. She'd chosen a bra to flatten an already flat chest. 'What's the point?' she asked, when Enid said she was going off to university. Couldn't she even see that?

Little Enid, so bright and knowledgeable and de-termined! So young, so ruthless – a warrior! And fortune favours the brave, the strong, the ruthless. That was the point. Enid's professor, Walter Walther, looked at Enid in a lingering way, and Enid looked straight back. Take me! Well, not quite take me. Love me now, take me eventually.

Walter Walther was forty-eight. Enid was nineteen. Enid was studying Chaucer. Enid said in an essay that Chaucer's Parfait Gentle Knight was no hero but a crude mercenary, and Chaucer, in his adulation, was being ironic; Walter Walther hadn't thought of that before, and at forty-eight it is delightful to meet someone who says something you haven't thought of before. And she was so young, and dewy, almost downy, so that if she was out in the rain the drops lay like silver balls upon her skin; and she was surprisingly knowledge-able for one so young, and knew all about music and painting, which Walter didn't, much, and she had an interesting, rich father, if a rather dowdy, vague, distant little mother. And Enid was warm.

Oh, Enid was warm! Enid was warm against his body on stolen nights. Walter's wife Rosanne, four years older than he, was over fifty. Rain fell off her like water off a duck's back – her skin being oily, not downy. Enid had met Rosanne once or twice baby-sitting; or rather adolescent-sitting, for Walter and Rosanne's two children, Barbara and Bernadette.

Rosanne didn't stand a chance against Enid. Enid still fought the old, old war, and Rosanne had put away her weapons long ago.

'He's so unhappy with his wife,' said Enid to Margot. 'She's such a cold unfeeling bitch. She's only interested in her career, not in him at all, or the children.' Margot was Enid's friend. Margot had owl eyes and a limpid handshake and not a hope of seducing, let alone winning, a married professor. But Margot understood Enid, and was a good friend to her, and had most of the qualities Enid's mother Patty had, and one more important one besides – self-doubt.

'Men never leave their wives for their mistresses,' warned Margot. It was a myth much put about, no doubt by wives, in the days of the Great War, to frighten the enemy. Enid knew better: she could tell a savage war mask from the frightened face of a foe in retreat. Enid knew Rosanne was frightened by the way she would follow Enid into the kitchen if Walter Walther was there alone, getting ice for drinks or scraping mud from the children's shoes.

Enid was pleased. A frightened foe seldom wins. The attacker is usually victorious, even if the advantage of surprise is gone, especially if the victim is old: Rosanne was old. She'd had the children late. It wasn't as if Walter Walther had really wanted children. He knew what kind of mother she'd make – cold.

Enid was warm. She knew how to silhouette her head against the sunlight so that her hair made a halo round her head, and then turn her face slowly so that the pure line of youth, the one that runs from ear to chin, showed to advantage. Rosanne had trouble with her back. Trouble with her back! Rosanne was a hag with one foot in the grave and with the iron bonds of matrimony would drag Walter Walther down there with her, if Walter didn't somehow break the bonds.

And Enid knew how to behave in bed, too: always keeping something in reserve, never taking the initiative, always the pupil, never the teacher. Enid had seen the *Art of Love* in Rosanne's bookshelves, and guessed her to be sexually experimental and innovatory. And she was later proved right, when Walter managed to voice one of his few actual complaints about his wife: there was, he felt, something indecent about Rosanne's sexual prowess: something disagreeably insatiable in her desires; it made Walter, from time to humiliating time, impotent.

Otherwise, it wasn't so much lack of love for
Rosanne that Walter suffered from, as surfeit of love
for Enid.

Enid exulted. And Rosanne was using worn-out old
weapons: that particular stage in the war had ended
long ago. The battle these days went to the innocent,
not to the experienced. Modern man, Enid knew by
instinct, especially those with a tendency to impotence,
requires docility in bed and admiration and exultation –
not excitement and exercise.

'He'll never leave the children,' said Margot. 'Men
don't.' But Enid had been left. Enid knew very well
that men did. And Barbara and Bernadette were not the
most lovable of children – how could they be? With
such a mother as Rosanne – a working mother who
never even remembered her children's birthdays, never
baked a cake, never ironed or darned, never cleaned
the oven? Rosanne was a translator with the Interna-
tional Cocoa Board – a genius at languages, but not at
motherhood. She was cold, stringy and sour – all the
things soft, warm, rounded Enid was not. Walter said
so, in bed, and increasingly out of it.

'What are you playing at?' asked Helene, crossly. Her
own attitude to the world was moderating. She was an old
retired warrior, sitting in a castle she'd won by force of
arms, shaking her head at the shockingness of war.

Patty now lived alone in a little council flat in
Birmingham. As Enid had left home Arthur no longer
paid Patty maintenance. Why should he?

'You want Walter because Walter's Rosanne's,'
observed Patty to Enid one day in a rare rush of

insight to the head. Patty's doctor had started giving her oestrogen for her hot flushes, and side-effects were beginning to show. There was a geranium in a pot on Patty's windowsill, when Enid went to break the news to her mother that Walter was finally leaving Rosanne. A geranium! Patty, who never could see the point in pot plants!

All the same, something, if only oestrogen, was now putting a sparkle in Patty's eye, and she turned up at Walter and Enid's wedding in a kind of velvet safari jacket which made her look almost sexy, and when Arthur crossed the room to speak to his ex-wife, she did not turn away, but actually saw the point of shaking his hand, and even laying her cheek against his, in affection and forgiveness.

Enid, in her white velvet trouser suit, saw: and a pang of almost physical pain roared through her, and for a second, just a second, looking at Walter, she saw not her great love but an elderly, paunchy, lecherous stranger. Even though he'd slimmed down quite remarkably during the divorce. It wasn't surprising! Rosanne had behaved like a bitch, and it had told on them both. Nevertheless, people remarked at the wedding that they'd never seen Walter looking so well – or Enid so elegant. He'd somehow scaled down to forty, and she up to thirty. Hardly a difference at all!

Barbara and Bernadette were bridesmaids. Rosanne had been against the idea, out of envy and malice mixed. She hadn't even been prepared to make their dresses, which Enid thought particularly spiteful. 'I'd never have made a bridesmaid's dress for you,' said Patty. 'Not to wear at your father's wedding.' 'That's altogether different,' said Enid, hurt and confused by the way Patty was seeing the war, almost as if she, Patty, were Rosanne's ally; more Helene's enemy than Enid's mother.

And then Helene upset her. 'I hope you're not thinking of having children,' she said, during the reception. 'Of course I am,' said Enid. 'Some men can't stand it,' said Helene. 'Your father, for one. Why do you think I never had any?' 'Well, I'm sure he could stand me,' said Enid, with a self-confidence she did not feel. For perhaps he just plain couldn't? Perhaps some of the blame for his departure was Enid's, not Patty's. Perhaps if she'd been nicer her father would never have left? And perhaps, indeed, he wouldn't!

Well, if we can't be nice, we can at least try to be perfect. Enid set out on her journey through life with perfection in mind. Doing better! Oh, how neat the corners of the beds she tucked, how fresh the butter, how crisp the tablecloth! Her curtains were always fully lined, her armpits smooth and washed, never merely sprayed. Enid never let her weapons get rusty. She would do better, thank you, than Patty, or Helene, or Rosanne.

Walter Walther clearly adored his Enid and let the world know it. His colleagues half envied, half pitied him. Walter would ring Enid from the department twice a day and talk baby-talk at her. Until recently he'd talked to his daughter Barbara in just such a manner. His colleagues came to the conclusion, over many a coffee table, that now the daughter had reached puberty the father, in marrying a girl of roughly the same age, was acting out incest fantasies too terrible to acknowledge. No one mentioned the word love: for this was the new language of the post-war age. If there was to be no hate, how could there be love?

In the meantime, for Walter and Enid, there was perpetual trouble with Rosanne. She insisted at first on staying in the matrimonial home, and it took a lawsuit and some fairly sharp accountants to drive her out: presently she lived with the girls in a little council flat. Oddly enough, it was rather like Patty's. Practical, but somehow depressing. 'You see,' said Enid. 'No gift for living! Poor Walter! What a terrible life she gave him.' In the Great War men gave women money, and women gave men life.

Barbara and Bernadette came to stay at weekends. They had their old rooms. Enid prettified them, and lined the curtains. She was a better mother to Barbara and Bernadette than Rosanne had ever been. Walter said so. Enid remembered their birthdays, and saw to their verrucas and had their hair styled. They looked at her with sullen gratitude, like slaves saved from slaughter.

Rosanne lost her job. Rosanne said – of course, it was because the responsibility of being a one-parent family and earning a living was too much for her, but Enid and Walter knew the loss of her job was just a simple matter of redundancy combined with lack of charm. Bernadette's asthma got worse. 'Of course the poor child's ill,' said Enid. 'With such a mother!' Enid

didn't believe in truces. She ignored white flags and
went in for the kill.

Enid had a pond built in the garden and entertained
Walter's friends on Campari and readings of Shake-
speare's sonnets. They were literary people, after all, or
claimed to be. 'Couldn't we do without the sonnets?'
said Walter.

But Enid insisted on the sonnets, and the friends drifted
away. 'It's Rosanne's doing,' said Enid. 'She's turned
them against us.' And she twined her white, soft, serpent's
arms round his grizzly, stranger body and he believed her.
His students, he noticed, seemed less respectful of him
than they had been: not as if he had grown younger but
they had grown older. Air came through the lecture-
room windows, on a hot summer's day, like a sigh. Well,
at least he was married, playing honestly and fair, unlike
his colleagues, who were for the most part hit-and-run
seducers. As for Rosanne, he knew she knew how to look
after herself. She always had. A man, in the Great War,
usually preferred a woman who couldn't.

'Let's have a baby of our own soon,' said Enid. A
baby! He hadn't thought of that. She was his baby. Or
was he hers?

'We're so happy,' said Enid. 'You and I. It doesn't
matter what the world thinks or says. We were just
both a little out of step, that's all, time-wise. God meant
us for each other. Don't you feel that?'

He queried her use of the word God, but otherwise
agreed with what she said. Her words came as definite
instruction from some powerful, knowledgeable
source. They flowed, unsullied by doubt. He, being

older, had to grope for meanings. He was too wise, and this could only diffuse his certainty, since wisdom is the acknowledgment of ignorance.

'Of course you should have a baby, Enid,' said Patty. 'Why not?' But she wasn't really thinking. She was having an affair with a mini-cab driver, and had forgotten about Enid. 'Your behaviour is obscene and disgusting,' Enid shouted at her mother. '*He's young.*'

'What's the point in your making all this fuss?' asked Patty. 'I deserve a little happiness in my life, and I'm sure you brought me precious little!'

Enid got pregnant, straight away. Walter went out and got drunk when he heard, with old friends of himself and Rosanne. Enid was so upset by this double disloyalty she went and stayed with her friend Margot for at least three days.

Margot was married and pregnant, too, and by one of Walter Walther's students, who had spots and bad breath. They lived on their grants, and beans and cider. Nevertheless, her husband went with her to the antenatal clinic and they pored over baby books together. Walter Walther took the view, common in the Great War, that the begetting of children was something to do with the one-upmanship of woman against woman, and very little to do with the man.

'Look, Enid,' said Walter, a new Walter, briskly and unkindly, 'you just get on with it by yourself.' Arthur had left Patty to get on with it by herself, too. Her very name, Enid, had been a last-minute choice by Patty with the registrar hovering over her hospital bed, because Arthur just left it to her.

'You can't have everything,' was what Helene said, when Enid murmured a complaint or two. 'You can't have status, money, adoration and what Margot has as well.'

'Why not?' demanded Enid. 'I want *everything!*'

Enid saw herself on a mountain top, a million women bowing down before her, acknowledging her victory. Her foot would be heavy on the necks of those she humbled. That was how it ought to be. She pulled herself together. She knew that, in the Great War, being pregnant could make you or break you. Great prizes were to be won – the best mother, the prettiest child, the whitest white – but much was risked. The enemy could swoop down, slenderwaisted and laughing and lively, and deliver any number of mortal wounds. So Enid wore her prettiest clothes, and sighed a little but never grunted when the baby lay on some pelvic nerve or other, and never let Walter suffer a moment because of what he had done to her. (In those pre-pill days men made women pregnant: women didn't just get pregnant.)

His boiled egg and toast soldiers and freshly milled coffee and the single flower in the silver vase were always there on the breakfast table at half past eight sharp and they'd eat together, companionably. Rosanne had slopped Sugar Puffs into bowls for the family breakfast, and they'd eaten among the uncleared children's homework and students' essays. Slut!

Walter was protective. 'We have to take extra special care of you,' he'd say, helping her across roads. But he seemed a little embarrassed. Something grated: she didn't know what. They ate in rather more often than before.

Then Rosanne, who ought by rights to have been lying punch-drunk in some obscure corner of the battlefield, rose up and delivered a nasty body-blow. Barbara and Bernadette were to come to live with Enid and Walter. Rosanne couldn't cope, in such crowded surroundings. She had a new job, and couldn't always be rushing home for Bernadette's asthma. Could she?

'A new boyfriend, more like,' said Walter, bitterly. Enid restrained from pointing out that Rosanne was an old, old woman with a bad back and hardly in the field for admirers.

Now six perfectly cooked boiled eggs on the table each morning – Bernadette and Barbara demanded two each – is twelve times as difficult to achieve as two. By the time the last one's in, the first one's cooked, but which one is it?

Walter looked at his bowl of Sugar Puffs one morning and said, 'Just like old times,' and the girls looked knowingly and giggled. They looked at Enid and her swelling tum with contempt and pity. They borrowed her clothes and her make-up. They refused to be taken to art galleries, or theatres; they refused even to play Monopoly, let alone Happy Families. They referred to their father as the Old Goat.

Sometimes she hated them. But Walter would not let her. 'Look,' said Walter, 'you did come along and disrupt their lives. You owe them something, at least.' As if it was all nothing to do with him. Which in a way it wasn't. It was between Rosanne and Enid.

Enid locked herself out of the house one day and, though she knew the girls were inside, when she knocked they wouldn't let her in. It was raining. Afterwards they just said they hadn't heard. And she'd fallen and hurt her knee trying to climb in the window, and might have lost the baby. Bernadette threw a bad asthma attack and got all the attention.

Walter spent more and more time in the department. She and he hardly made love at all any more. It didn't seem right.

Enid went into labour at eight o'clock one evening. She rang Walter Walther at the English Department where he said he was, but he wasn't. She rang Margot and wept, and Margot said, 'I don't think I've ever known you cry, Enid,' and Margot's spotty husband said, 'You'll probably find him round at Rosanne's. I wouldn't tell you, if it wasn't an emergency.'

'Yes,' said Barbara and Bernadette. 'He goes round to see Mum quite a lot. We didn't like to tell you because we didn't want to upset you.

'Really,' they said, 'the whole thing was a plot to get rid of us. The thing is, neither of them can stand us.' (Barbara and Bernadette went to one of the large new comprehensive schools, where there were pupil-counsellors, who could explain everything and anything, and were never lost for words.)

Enid screamed and wept all through her labour, not just from pain. They'd never known a noisier mother, they said: and she'd been so quiet and elegant and self-controlled throughout her pregnancy.

Enid gave birth to a little girl. Now in the Great War, the birth of a girl was, understandably, and unlike now, cause for commiseration rather than rejoicing.

Nevertheless, Enid rejoiced. And in so doing, abandoned a battle which was really none of her making; she laid down her arms: she kissed her mother and Helene when they came to visit her, clasped her baby and admitted weakness and distress to Barbara and Bernadette, who actually then seemed quite to like her.

Walter Walther did not come home. He stayed with Rosanne. Enid, Barbara and Bernadette lived in the same house, shared suspender belts, shampoo and boyfriends, and looked after baby Belinda. Walter and Rosanne visited, sheepishly, from time to time, and sent money. Enid went back to college and took a degree in psychology, and was later to earn a good living as a research scientist.

Later still she was to become something of a propagandist in the new cold war against men; she wore jeans and a donkey jacket and walked round linked arm-in-arm with women. But that was, perhaps, hardly surprising, so treacherous had the old male allies turned out to be. All the same, yesterday's enemy, tomorrow's friend! Who is to say what will happen next?

1982

Subject to Diary

If you do nothing unexpected, nothing unexpected happens.

Oriole Green gave her name to the clinic receptionist, an unsmiling girl with dark skin and blonde hair and almost no eyebrows at all, who punched Oriole's name up on the computer and then asked her if she'd been to the clinic before. Oriole said yes, without thinking, for she was under considerable stress, and the girl with no eyebrows punched some more buttons and then said flatly, 'You're lying. You haven't.'

Oriole was on the eve of her fortieth birthday and for fifteen years had been spoken to, on the whole, and at least out of the bedroom, with politeness and respect. Though in the bedroom, she had noticed, men who were most – no, reverential was the wrong word, as was courteous; guarded was perhaps more accurate – were the ones who most wished to take her down a peg or so: called her names, slapped her around a little. Oriole didn't mind: it was a relief. It was the price, she reckoned, a woman paid for being successful. Nothing was for nothing.

But this was not a bedroom. This was not a suitor, an impregnator, an erotic hit-and-runner, this was a chit of a fat-faced girl behind a desk in the Serena Clinic for Women, a double-fronted house in a dusty suburban garden where pregnancies were terminated for money, and such a girl, who was doubtless paid twice what her equivalent in the public sector would be, should not feel entitled to be rude to clients. The girl wore a pink name-tag on her white coat. It read 'Daisy'. Daisy should smile and be friendly and helpful; and out of human kindness, what's more, not merely in the interest of good public relations. Except, Oriole supposed, a girl in her early twenties who was not pregnant, who was not a supplicant for termination, would feel superior to her less fortunate sisters. Or perhaps, more likely, since the waiting list at the clinic was long, the problem was merely that no one had bothered properly to train the reception staff. Even in the private sector, termination came under the heading 'seller's market'.

'I must have made a mistake,' said Oriole, returning rudeness with courtesy, as one should. She had most certainly been to the Serena Clinic twice before, only, of course, as she would have remembered sooner had she not been under stress, using another name on each occasion. On her first visit, when she was 28, she had given her married name, and on the second, when she was 36, her boyfriend's surname, out of some kind of rivalry, she now supposed, with his wife. At the time she had just felt better using his name, not her own. But now she had given the clinic her own original name, her school and professional name: as if finally she accepted responsibility, not for a child exactly, but at least for the non-event the child must of necessity be: and she felt less somehow hole-in-corner, in fact rather open and brave.

Even 'child' sounded wrong. A putative non-child perhaps: an alleged and accidental non-child. Of course this non-child, this growing cluster of cells, had in a way to be congratulated, inasmuch as, so successfully and so far, it had evaded all the powerful suggestions that it should not be, should not come into existence, egg and sperm by some miracle of happenstance colliding and joining, the two amongst millions not to succumb to the hazards set up by nature itself – a too acid, too alkali womb: a too early, too late arrival of the egg and/or delivery of the sperm: and so forth; oh, well done, well done! Not to mention the more considered incentives towards not-to-be: the contraceptive poisons, the rubber sheaths, the hormone-induced non-receptivity, the other many traps and fail-safe devices invented by humanity to stop itself breeding itself out of existence. What, survived all this? Still living? And then, once fertilized, to have clung on satisfactorily; to have successfully set the welcoming mechanism of the host body into vigorous motion – oh yes, you had to congratulate this cluster of dividing cells, even as your own surging hormones sickened you.

Well done, well done, you had to say, for having got so far! But also, so sorry, I do have to hit you on the head at this the last and greatest hurdle. I don't want you. You can't survive if I don't want you. You got it right, but in the wrong body. A factor beyond your comprehension: one you were too tiny to comprehend, let alone forestall. That the whole great intended unit should notice you as you grew, and turn against you. For now that your scale has changed other forces must come into play. Pipped at the post, oh brave and courageous one, the one amongst millions. What was the month now? June? Left to itself it would be born in November.

'Funny thing to make a mistake about,' said Daisy uncheerily. She had a hairy upper lip, and had bleached the dark hairs, which was a mistake. Why didn't she just tweeze them out? 'Sit down,' said fat-faced, greasy Daisy, as if Oriole's standing was in itself a nuisance.

Oriole sat down. There was one other person in the waiting room, which was painted pale pink and had pictures on the walls of pretty ladies in crinolines, in silhouette. She was a thin girl with a white face and red-rimmed eyes, who lowered her eyes to her copy of *House and Garden* rather than meet Oriole's. There was an article inside the magazine, Oriole knew, in the series 'Successful Women', featuring Oriole Green. Oriole had cut it out and pinned it on her kitchen wall. She was proud of it. The thin girl flicked past the page.

Oriole had been named for a bird, so her mother said: born to soar and fly. Of course you succeed, said her mother, proudly. Sometimes Oriole felt like a bird: she had a lean, small, muscly body covered by the finest designer feathers, a small beaky nose and bright sharp intelligent eyes, and a lot of reddish hair: she could feel herself sometimes hopping about: this appointment, that appointment, up those stairs, down that lift, pecking around, then soaring, soaring –

There was an uncomfortable silence in the waiting room. The thin girl snivelled, and lit up a cigarette.

Oriole took out her diary and looked through November. It was a busy month. Ex-King Alleyne of a minor Arab state had his book coming out: the Shrinks were making a come-back: there was the Head Office Conference in Reykjavik: all fourteen branches would be represented. She, Oriole Green, personnel manager, would be speaking. In December the company was going public. You had to prepare people for change, even if change was to their advantage people hated it; hers was to be the key-note speech. How could you fit in having a baby with all that, even if you wanted one, loved the father? Neither of which she did, not for lack of trying. How could you find a man to love; a man who was altogether admirable and superior to yourself, once you were past, say, thirty, and earning well? And you didn't have babies by, marry or set up home with men you didn't love. Did you? Others seemed to, it was true, but only women with no standards, no expectations, no subtlety.

Oriole couldn't remember waiting like this, on previous occasions. She'd been shown immediately to her room, undressed, settled down, been weighed up by the anaesthetist and gone straight into surgery. She felt obscurely that the wait was Daisy's fault.

Oriole flicked through the current week. She had managed to adjust her appointments to keep not only this afternoon free but tomorrow morning as well. Body and mind might need a little time to recover, to adjust to a change in state. She reckoned to feel low for a week or so in any case. The sooner the operation was done the better. Hours counted. This particular hour was somehow dripping uncontrolled out of her life, thanks to Daisy.

The pale girl and her suitcase were taken away by a nurse whose name-tag said 'Audrey'. Daisy and Audrey, the girls who worked at the clinic. Audrey smiled a great deal, showing broken teeth. Audrey's smile was worse than Daisy's unsmile. Were the Serena Clinic forward-looking, it would have had Audrey's teeth capped. Or not employed her at all. The sense of things rotten or bad or missing in such a place as this surely had at all costs to be avoided.

'Will it be long?' Oriole asked Daisy, rashly.

Daisy looked back at Oriole and thought unspeakable things or so it seemed to Oriole. Oriole was, quite determinedly, not looking her best. She wore no eye make-up. People went either way at funerals, she noticed. They either looked their best or their worst. 'Enjoy it while you can,' said Daisy.

Oriole had worn her best to her father's funeral: her worst to her mother's. She wondered why. She hadn't grieved over-much when either of them died; she thought perhaps because she loved them, and so felt little guilt, and their deaths were after all timely. Her father had gone suddenly, through a stroke. Her mother lingered on in a kind of passive shock for less than a year, then had cancer of the liver diagnosed, and died promptly and painlessly almost of her own volition. They'd been in their seventies, and neither had enjoyed it. They were accustomed to being active, and were not so short-sighted they couldn't see the litter on the floor, the bits of stick and wrappers that the dog chewed up, which they were now too stiff to bend to pick up; they had to wait for the daily help to arrive to see to it. Old age was no way to end a life. If you had a diary for a whole life, all the appointments would be crammed near the beginning: getting fewer and fewer as you flicked through, until the pages were all but empty.

Oriole felt tears in her eyes. She knew Daisy would misconstrue them. Daisy did. Daisy said, 'Sometimes people change their minds – ' but she said it unpleasantly; judgementally, Oriole thought, she who had been named after a bird, to soar and sing and rejoice. The kind of women who end up in this waiting room of mine are feckless and hopeless, Daisy implied: the kind who change their minds and put me and my computer to endless trouble.

Oriole smiled coolly at Daisy and made no reply.

Oriole thought, well, this is really not time wasted. Thank you, Daisy. This is thinking time, reflective time. Everyone needs this quality time. In progressive businesses such spare time is built into timescales, just as free periods were when we were at school. No doubt that particular free time was the result of timetabling inconsistencies and inadequacies. Never mind: we students, being ignorant, interpreted it as a gift, a kindness, from a benign authority and were the happier for it.

Seven weeks from her last period. She looked that up in her diary too. There was the little tick. Regular as clockwork; predictable as the moon. Was the moon predictable? She supposed so. The moon came and went, waxed and waned, without Oriole noticing. What was the point of noticing the moon, if the moon took no notice of you? 'Oriole,' her mother once said, 'life is not all give and take, tit for tat: you do this and I'll do that, watch my back and I'll watch yours. Other factors intervene.' But what? Love? Her mother loved her father and she, Oriole, had intervened by being born. And even love ended in death, in silence. In strokes and cancer of the liver.

So little time to think. Too tired to think when she got home: and for holidays she'd go to health hydros where she'd starve and exercise herself into somewhere between a stupor and a high. Too tired to talk. And who was there to talk to, even if you could formulate the right words to echo the bizarreness of your thoughts? By the time you'd said too often to too many friends, when they rang to suggest lunch, or an outing, or a holiday, 'Just a moment, I'll get out my diary,' and then, 'Sorry, I can't make it,' they'd lost patience, moved on, thought you valued something more than them. Which in a way you did, so you could hardly blame them. Men in business had wives to live their lives for them: remember birthdays, arrange dinners, have their children: Oriole only had herself.

She'd been married once: but it hadn't outlasted a year. He'd been an air-traffic controller: he knew exactly where not only he but everything and everyone else would be, ought to be, at a certain time: in the end the uncertainty of her hours, the sudden crises, the middle-of-the-night phone calls – some of her clients were Australians, and just didn't seem to comprehend that their glorious midday was someone else's exhausted two in the morning – had defeated him. 'We're heading for a crash,' he'd said, panicky, and so of course they were. He wanted her to be at home when he was, waiting, coming into existence when he opened the front door, blanking out of it when he left. Well, of course, she wanted him to be the same. There when she wanted him: not when she didn't. Francis, her husband.

She'd felt bad about failing to meet his demands, and confused by his expectations. She couldn't concentrate, she'd quite forgotten to look in her diary. Francis had been the one to point out that she hadn't bled for two months. She was three months gone by the time she got to the Serena Clinic. That had been really horrible. And when she got back four days later there were two significant messages on the answerphone: one on Monday asking her to be a fill-in speaker at the Toronto conference – and she knew her promotion depended upon it – and one on Wednesday from Francis saying he knew she would go to Toronto, not stay at home, and so he was going off himself. Where? Anywhere, just somewhere else, away from her. And so he had. Now he was married to a nice

boring little stay-at-home and had two children. The
elder one had been born with some disorder which
made its head swell up with water – Oriole somehow
felt it was her fault, though of course that was absurd.
But she'd been upset. She'd loved him, this man who
had the flying machines within his care and control –
this dextrous male. If he'd given her time she could
have broken the addiction, because that was what it
was, an addiction to her diary. Subject to diary. The
diary that kept you forgetful, so busy you were being
reminded. Forgetful of what?

She couldn't remember now why she'd felt obliged
to get rid of the air controller's baby. Some necessity,
some need, some fear? Perhaps his. Or had she just
been putting motherhood off to some more convenient time? If that had been the reason, she'd been wise
enough. If she looked through past diaries it was clear
there never had been, never would be, a convenient
time.

Speaking the unspeakable. Daisy was punching up
names and numbers on her computer. She could say to
her, 'Daisy' – such an advantage to the anonymous, the
habit of putting name-tags on the humble – 'Daisy,
why do you pluck out your eyebrows but leave your
lip-hairs alone? Shouldn't it be the other way round?'
But you couldn't say that. Not just because Daisy could
pull a string or two, make sure Oriole's anaesthetic was
too light, expose her to the risk of septicaemia and
other foreseeable things as well – the humble had all
kinds of amazing powers – but because it was not done
to say things to people which would hurt in the short

term though help in the long. A pity. She searched for
something friendly and companionable to say to Daisy,
but failed.

What could she say? 'I am an important person;
please treat me with courtesy'? No. Any woman with
her legs apart and some tearing, rending instrument up
inside her as she slapped nature in the face was pretty
much of a muchness with the last one on the table, the
next one to come.

'You are here on the computer,' said Daisy, 'if
Green's your maiden name?'

'Yes,' said Oriole. Maiden name. How sweet and
naive it sounded. She wondered what kind of girl she'd
been. How could one ever know: you could only see
yourself from the inside out. She thought she probably
hadn't ever had much brain, only competence and a
kind of soaring sensuality. So how had it gone wrong?
Was it mood, a kind of generalized feeling tone, or
nature, or just the chance events of a certain day which
had led her to this point: forty, childless, unmarried.
Not a bad point to be. Nothing wrong with being
forty, or childless, or unmarried, except that spoken all
together they sounded too final, too unwanted for
comfort.

'The first time you were here you let it go three
months,' observed Daisy, 'and there were complications. Still, it hasn't affected your fertility.'

'Clearly not,' said Oriole. The second time she'd
been only six weeks' pregnant: that was Hassan's baby.
She remembered well enough why she'd let that one
go by. Hassan had been beautiful, beautiful, but

married: he didn't think, or reason, or plan: he couldn't organize anything: he was a gardener: he loved all living, growing things except, it seemed, Oriole's baby. She didn't want to lose him so she'd lost the baby instead: she never even told him. She lost him anyway. He worked for the Parks Department, nine to five, and the complications of her unsocial hours and his getting away in secret from his wife had quite worn out the romance. Lovers looked silly in diaries: their initials softly pencilled in. 'I will meet you, my darling, my darling, subject to diary!' Men could do it: women couldn't: that was the problem.

'An expensive form of contraception, if you ask me,' said Daisy. 'I didn't ask you,' said Oriole.

She could see this was her last chance. But how did you have a baby by your PA and go on working in the same office with him? Stop work and live off what? With him? Off him? On his lower salary? He wouldn't get much further up the ladder: she wrote his annual report: she knew it well enough. Oriole Green, a source of scandal and mirth! Oriole? Oh, Oriole the high-flyer: flew over a volcano, got her wings burned, plummeted, died. Babies got into your heart and twisted knives of guilt and obligation. Babies killed you: everything in you that wasn't totally female, at any rate. That flourished, to the detriment of the whole.

'Sorry I spoke. No need to snap,' said Daisy. 'Everyone snaps in here. It's the stress.'

And what you knew you grew to need, couldn't do without. The luxury of her bedroom: with its view over the city: the sense that it honoured you, found you special: the routine of early morning: the private, leisured silk, carefully chosen, against the skin: the softness of pale carpet; again yet softer, paler feet as you searched with your toe for your slipper, warm and safe inside while wind and rain and nature pattered against the pane. She didn't want to give it up. Other people, men, babies, intruded into the eroticism of solitude. Perhaps you had to get married before you were twenty, have babies before you were twenty-five, before you knew what there was to miss.

'Are you really nearly forty?' asked Daisy, looking across from her computer screen, 'because you don't look it.' Oriole smiled coldly; perhaps this impossible Daisy was a temp: filling in for someone who must surely know how to behave, and understood without being told that the personal information now freely available about everything and everyone to any girl with a computer at her fingertips had somehow, in the interests of the social niceties, to be referred to but at the same time tactfully overlooked.

'Mind you,' said Daisy, 'we get people in here up to fifty, but mostly they've got six already and it's medical. Lots of women have babies at forty.'

'More fool them,' said Oriole shortly: she would have stayed silent if it weren't for the sudden flow of words from Daisy's hairy mouth which filled the pale-pink room in a dangerous way, and might break the silence for ever if they were not somehow stilled. It didn't work.

'There are tests for Down's Syndrome,' went on Daisy, 'if that's what you're worrying about.'

'I hadn't even considered it,' said Oriole. Nor had she. A non-child cannot have Down's Syndrome or, if it does, can hardly suffer from feelings of inadequacy on that account; not during its brief putative existence.

'Lots do,' said Daisy. 'You'd be surprised. It isn't a nice job, this: but if I don't do it someone worse will.'

'It seems perfectly reasonable work to me,' said Oriole. 'I imagine there is a high degree of job satisfaction. You're working in the community, with people, in a healing environment, meeting very important human needs.'

'Is that what I'm doing?' asked Daisy. 'It seems to me I'm working for a crew of murderers and not even getting danger money.'

'What sort of danger?' asked Oriole, startled.

'Being hated,' said Daisy. 'People just sit where you're sitting, waiting, beaming out their dislike.'

'Perhaps it comes from the babies,' said Oriole, before she had time to think. 'Perhaps the hostility comes from them. They can hardly thank you for what you're doing. Well, not doing. But for helping organize the doing. That is to say the doing-away-with.'

'Oh thank you,' said Daisy. 'That's a real help. Ta very much.' She swung her swivel chair so that her back was to Oriole. Her hair was greasy. There was a yellowy stain down the back of her white coat.

Oriole thought, this is me, Oriole Green, sitting in a female clinic having a spat with a greasy girl at a computer. This is where love leads you: or sex, while it lasts. And of course it wouldn't last, couldn't. The gap between affairs lengthened: she noticed it. Once one lover trod hard upon the heels of the last: now years could intervene: the diary of love had long, long stretches of nothingness. Last chance, last chance. She might still find someone like herself, intolerably busy, to settle down with, subject to diary, to provide a baby with a proper home but, come to think of it, she doubted it. Last chance!

'Daisy,' said Oriole, 'there's a yellowy stain down the back of your overall. I only mention it because you can't see it, and I expect your employers put quite a price on smartness.'

'They put a price on murder,' said Daisy, 'Nothing else. I could wear a butcher's overall for all they cared. Bloodstains and all. How much are they asking you, Oriole?' She consulted the screen. 'Eight hundred and twelve pounds plus anaesthetic fees. Wow! Of course, you are forty. That puts the insurance premiums up. Most women get out at about six hundred. No reduction for quantity, it seems, or you'd be less. And the stains down the back of my overall will be baby sick. And my own view is if you have a baby you should stay home and look after it, but chance would be a fine thing, wouldn't it?'

'Chance,' said Oriole, wings healed, spirits soaring, 'is a very, very fine thing,' and when the smiling nurse with broken teeth came in to take her and her overnight suitcase up to her room, she said she'd changed her mind.

'You'll lose your deposit,' said the nurse, her smile simply blanking out, not even fading. 'Your room being booked, and the operating theatre too. We can't rebook at this late stage. These last-minute changes of mind are very inconsiderate of others. And we've had a whole spate of them lately.' The nurse looked very hard at Daisy, knowing perfectly well whose fault it was, but Daisy had fallen sullen and silent again and didn't so much as raise her eyes from the screen.

As for Oriole, she asked for a year's leave of absence on full pay and got it, with no argument from anyone. If you do the unexpected, unexpected things happen.

1989

Ind Aff or Out of Love in Sarajevo

This is a sad story. It has to be. It rained in Sarajevo, and we had expected fine weather.

The rain filled up Sarajevo's pride, two footprints set into a pavement, marking the spot where the young assassin Princip stood to shoot the Archduke Ferdinand and his wife. (Don't forget his wife: everyone forgets his wife, the Archduchess.) That happened in the summer of 1914. Sarajevo is a pretty town, Balkan style, mountain-rimmed. A broad, swift, shallow river runs through its centre, carrying the mountain snows away. The river is arched by many bridges and the one nearest the two footprints has been named The Princip Bridge. The young man is a hero in these parts. Not only does he bring in the tourists – look, look, the spot, the very spot! – but by his action, as everyone knows, he lit the spark which fired the timber which caused World War I which crumbled the Austro–Hungarian Empire, the crumbling of which made modern Yugoslavia possible. Forty million dead (or was it thirty?), but who cares? So long as he loved his country.

The river, they say, can run so shallow in the summer it's known derisively as 'the wet road'. To-day, from what I could see through the sheets of falling rain, it seemed full enough. Yugoslavian streets are always busy – no one stays home if they can help it (thus can an indecent shortage of housing space create a sociable nation) and it seemed that as if by common consent a shield of bobbing umbrellas had been erected two metres high to keep the rain off the streets. But the shield hadn't worked around Princip's corner, that was plain.

'Come all this way,' said Peter, who was a Professor of Classical History, 'and you can't even see the footprints properly, just two undistinguished puddles.' Ah, but I loved him. I shivered for his disappointment. He was supervising my thesis on varying concepts of morality and duty in the early Greek states as evidenced in their poetry and drama. I was dependent upon him for my academic future. Peter said I had a good mind but not a first-class mind, and somehow I didn't take it as an insult. I had a feeling first-class minds weren't all that good in bed.

Sarajevo is in Bosnia, in the centre of Yugoslavia, that grouping of unlikely states, that distillation of languages into the phonetic reasonableness of Serbo–Croat. We'd sheltered from the rain in an ancient mosque in Serbian Belgrade: done the same in a monastery in Croatia: now we spent a wet couple of days in Sarajevo beneath other people's umbrellas. We planned to go on to Montenegro, on the coast, where the fish and the artists come from, to swim and lie in the sun, and recover from the exhaustion caused by the sexual and moral torments of the last year. It couldn't possibly go on raining for ever. Could it? Satellite pictures showed black cloud swishing gently all over Europe, over the Balkans, into Asia – practically all the way from Moscow to London, in fact. It wasn't that Peter and I were being singled out. No. It was raining on his wife, too, back in Cambridge.

Peter was trying to make the decision, as he had been for the past year, between his wife and myself as his permanent life partner. To this end we had gone away, off the beaten track, for a holiday: if not with his wife's blessing, at least with her knowledge. Were we really, truly suited? We had to be sure, you see, that this was more than just any old professor-student romance: that it was the Real Thing, because the longer the indecision went on the longer Mrs Piper, Peter said, would be left dangling in uncertainty and distress. He and she had been married for twenty-four years; they'd stopped loving each other a long time ago, naturally – but there would be a fearful personal and practical upheaval entailed if he decided to leave permanently and shack up, as he put it, with me. Which I wanted him to do, because I loved him. And so far I was winning hands down. It didn't seem much of a contest at all, in fact. I'd been cool and thin and informed on the seat next to him in a Zagreb theatre (Mrs Piper was sweaty and only liked TV), was now eager and anxious for social and political instruction in Sarajevo (Mrs Piper spat in the face of knowledge, Peter had once told me), and planned to be lissom and topless – I hadn't quite decided: it might be counterproductive to underline the age differential – while I splashed and shrieked like a bathing belle in the shallows of the craggy Croatian coast (Mrs Piper was a swimming coach: I imagined she smelt permanently of chlorine).

So far as I could see it was no contest at all between his wife and myself. How could he possibly choose her while I was on offer? But Peter liked to luxuriate in guilt and indecision. And I loved him with an inordinate affection, and indulged him in this luxury.

Princip's footprints are a metre apart, placed like the feet of a modern cop on a training shoot-out – the left in front at a slight outward angle, the right behind, facing forward. There seemed great energy focused here. Both hands on the gun, run, stop, plant the feet, aim, fire! I could see the footprints well enough, in spite of Peter's complaint. They were clear enough to me, albeit puddled.

We went to a restaurant for lunch, since it was too wet to do what we loved to do: that is, buy bread, cheese, sausage, wine and go off somewhere in our hired car, into the woods or the hills, and picnic and make love. It was a private restaurant – Yugoslavia went over to a mixed capitalist-communist economy years back, so you get either the best or the worst of both systems, depending on your mood – that is to say, we knew we would pay more but be given a choice. We chose the wild boar.

'Probably ordinary pork soaked in red cabbage water to darken it,' said Peter. He was not in a good mood.

Cucumber salad was served first.

'Everything in this country comes with cucumber salad,' complained Peter. I noticed I had become used to his complaining. I supposed that when you had been married a while you simply wouldn't hear it. He was forty-six and I was twenty-five.

'They grow a lot of cucumber,' I said.

'If they can grow cucumbers,' Peter then asked, 'why can't they grow mange-tout?' It seemed a why-can't-they-eat-cake sort of argument to me, but not knowing enough about horticulture not to be out-flanked if I debated the point, I moved the subject on to safer ground.

'I suppose Princip's action couldn't really have started World War One,' I remarked. 'Otherwise, what a thing to have on your conscience! One little shot and the deaths of thirty million on your shoulders.'

'Forty,' he corrected me. Though how they reckon these things and get them right I can't imagine. 'Of course Princip didn't start the war. That's just a simple tale to keep the children quiet. It takes more than an assassination to start a war. What happened was that the build-up of political and economic tensions in the Balkans was such that it had to find some release.'

'So it was merely the shot that lit the spark that fired the timber that started the war, et cetera?'

'Quite,' he said. 'World War One would have had to have started sooner or later.'

'A bit later or a bit sooner', I said, 'might have made the difference of a million or so: if it was you on the battlefield in the mud and the rain you'd notice: exactly when they fired the starting-pistol: exactly when they blew the final whistle. Is that what they do when a war ends: blow a whistle? So that everyone just comes in from the trenches?'

But he wasn't listening. He was parting the flesh of the soft collapsed orangey-red pepper which sat in the middle of his cucumber salad; he was carefully extracting the pips. He didn't like eating pepper pips. His Nan had once told him they could never be digested, would stick to the wall of his stomach and do terrible damage. I loved him for his vulnerability, the bit of him that was forever little boy: I loved him for his dexterity and patience with his knife and fork. I'd finished my salad yonks ago, pips and all. I was hungry. I wanted my wild boar.

Peter might have been forty-six but he was six foot two and well-muscled and grizzled with it, in a dark-eyed, intelligent, broad-jawed kind of way. I adored him. I loved to be seen with him. 'Muscular-academic, not weedy-academic,' as my younger sister Clare once said. 'Muscular-academic is just a generally superior human being: everything works well from the brain to the toes. Weedy-academic is when there isn't enough vital energy in the person, and the brain drains all the strength from the other parts.' Well, Clare should know. Clare is only twenty-three, but of the superior human kind herself, vividly pretty, bright and competent – somewhere behind a heavy curtain of vibrant, as they say, red hair, which she only parts for effect. She had her first degree at twenty. Now she's married to a Harvard Professor of Economics seconded to the United Nations. She can even cook. I gave up competing when she was fourteen and I was sixteen. Though she too is capable of self-deception. I would say her husband was definitely of the weedy-academic rather than the muscular-academic type. And they have to live in Brussels.

The Archduke's chauffeur had lost his way, and was parked on the corner trying to recover his nerve when Princip came running out of a café, planted his feet, aimed and fired. Princip was seventeen – too young to hang. But they sent him to prison for life and, since he had TB to begin with, he only lasted three years. He died in 1917, in a Swiss prison. Or perhaps it was more than TB: perhaps they gave him a hard time, not learning till later, when the Austro-Hungarian Empire collapsed, that he was a hero. Poor Princip, too young to die – like so many other millions. Dying for love of a country.

'I love you,' I said to Peter, my living man, progenitor already of three children by his chlorinated, swimming-coach wife.

'How much do you love me?'

'Inordinately! I love you with inordinate affection.'

It was a joke between us. Ind Aff!

'Inordinate affection is a sin,' he'd told me. 'According to the Wesleyans. John Wesley himself worried about it to such a degree that he ended up abbreviating it in his diaries. Ind Aff. He maintained that what he felt for young Sophy, the eighteen-year-old in his congregation, was not Ind Aff, which bears the spirit away from God towards the flesh: no, what he felt was a pure and spiritual, if passionate, concern for Sophy's soul.'

Peter said now, as we waited for our wild boar, and he picked over his pepper, 'Your Ind Aff is my wife's sorrow, that's the trouble.' He wanted, I knew, one of the long half wrangles, half soul-sharings that we could keep going for hours, and led to piercing pains in the heart which could only be made better in bed. But our bedroom at the Hotel Europa was small and dark and looked out into the well of the building – a punishment room if ever there was one. (Reception staff did sometimes take against us.) When Peter had tried to change it in his quasi-Serbo-Croat, they'd shrugged their Bosnian shoulders and pretended not to understand, so we'd decided to put up with it. I did not fancy pushing hard single beds together – it seemed easier not to have the pain in the heart in the first place.

'Look,' I said, 'this holiday is supposed to be just the two of us, not Mrs Piper as well. Shall we talk about something else?'

Do not think that the Archduke's chauffeur was merely careless, an inefficient chauffeur, when he took the wrong turning. He was, I imagine, in a state of shock, fright and confusion. There had been two previous attempts on the Archduke's life since the cavalcade had entered town. The first was a bomb which got the car in front and killed its driver. The second was a shot, fired by none other than young Princip, which had missed. Princip had vanished into the crowd and gone to sit down in a corner café, where he ordered coffee to calm his nerves. I expect his hand trembled at the best of times – he did have TB. (Not the best choice of assassin, but no doubt those who arrange these things have to make do with what they can get.) The Archduke's chauffeur panicked, took the wrong road, realized what he'd done, and stopped to await rescue and instructions just, as it happened, outside the café where Princip sat drinking his coffee.

'What shall we talk about?' asked Peter, in even less of a good mood.

'The collapse of the Austro–Hungarian Empire?' I suggested. 'How does an Empire collapse? Is there no money to pay the military or the police, so everyone goes home? Or what?' He liked to be asked questions.

'The Hungro–Austrian Empire,' said Peter to me, 'didn't so much collapse as fail to exist any more. War destroys social organizations. The same thing happened after World War Two. There being no organizing bodies left between Moscow and London – and for London read Washington, then as now – it was left to these two to put in their own puppet governments. Yalta, 1994. It's taken the best part of forty-five years for nations of Western and Eastern Europe to remember who they are.'

'Austro–Hungarian,' I said, 'not Hungro–Austrian.'

'I didn't say Hungro–Austrian,' he said.

'You did,' I said.

'Didn't,' he said. 'What the hell are they doing about our wild boar? Are they out in the hills shooting it?'

My sister Clare had been surprisingly understanding about Peter. When I worried about him being older, she pooh-poohed it; when I worried about him being married, she said, 'Just go for it, sister. If you can unhinge a marriage, it's ripe for unhinging; it would happen sooner or later; it might as well be you. See a catch, go ahead and catch! Go for it!'

Princip saw the Archduke's car parked outside, and went for it. Second chances are rare in life: they must be responded to. Except perhaps his second chance was missing in the first place? He could have taken his cue from fate, and just sat and finished his coffee, and gone home to his mother. But what's a man to do when he loves his country? Fate delivered the Archduke into his hands: how could he resist it? A parked car, a uniformed and medalled chest, the persecutor of his country – how could Princip, believing God to be on his side, not see this as His intervention, push his coffee aside and leap to his feet?

Two waiters stood idly by and watched us waiting for our wild boar. One was young and handsome in a mountainous Bosnian way – flashing eyes, hooked nose, luxuriant black hair, sensuous mouth. He was about my age. He smiled. His teeth were even and white. I smiled back and, instead of the pain in the heart I'd become accustomed to as an erotic sensation, now felt, quite violently, an associated yet different pang which got my lower stomach. The true, the real pain of Ind Aff!

'Fancy him?' asked Peter.

'No,' I said. 'I just thought if I smiled the wild boar might come quicker.'

The other waiter was older and gentler: his eyes were soft and kind. I thought he looked at me reproachfully. I could see why. In a world which for once, after centuries of savagery, was finally full of young men, unslaughtered, what was I doing with this man with thinning hair?

'What are you thinking of?' Professor Piper asked me. He liked to be in my head.

'How much I love you,' I said automatically, and was finally aware how much I lied. 'And about the Archduke's assassination,' I went on, to cover the kind of tremble in my head as I came to my senses, 'and let's not forget his wife, she died too – how can you say World War One would have happened anyway? If Princip hadn't shot the Archduke something else, some undisclosed, unsuspected variable, might have come along and defused the whole political/military situation, and neither World War One nor Two would ever have happened. We'll just never know, will we?'

I had my passport and my traveller's cheques with me. (Peter felt it was less confusing if we each paid our own way.) I stood up, and took my raincoat from the peg.

'Where are you going?' he asked, startled.

'Home,' I said. I kissed the top of his head, where it was balding. It smelt gently of chlorine, which may have come from thinking about his wife so much, but might merely have been because he'd taken a shower that morning. ('The water all over Yugoslavia, though safe to drink, is unusually highly chlorinated': guide book.) As I left to catch a taxi to the airport the younger of the two waiters emerged from the kitchen with two piled plates of roasted wild boar, potatoes duchesse, and stewed peppers. ('Yugoslavian diet is unusually rich in proteins and fats': guide book.) I could tell from the glisten of oil that the food was no longer hot, and I was not tempted to stay, hungry though I was. Thus fate – or was it Bosnian wilfulness? – confirmed the wisdom of my intent.

And that was how I fell out of love with my professor, in Sarajevo, a city to which I am grateful to this day, though I never got to see much of it, because of the rain.

It was a silly sad thing to do, in the first place, to confuse mere passing academic ambition with love: to try and outdo my sister Clare. (Professor Piper was spiteful, as it happened, and did his best to have my thesis refused, but I went to appeal, which he never thought I'd dare to do, and won. I had a first-class mind after all.) A silly sad episode, which I regret. As silly and sad as Princip, poor young man, with his feverish mind, his bright tubercular cheeks, and his inordinate affection for his country, pushing aside his cup of coffee, leaping to his feet, taking his gun in both hands, planting his feet, aiming and firing – one, two, three shots and starting World War I. The first one missed, the second got the wife (never forget the wife), and the third got the Archduke and a whole generation, and their children, and their children's children, and on and on for ever. If he'd just hung on a bit, there in Sarajevo that August day, he might have come to his senses. People do, sometimes quite quickly.

1988

Down the Clinical Disco

You never know where you'll meet your own true love. I met mine down the clinical disco. That's him over there, the thin guy with the jeans, the navy jumper and the red woolly cap. He looks pretty much like anyone else, don't you think? That's hard work on his part, not to mention mine, but we got there in the end. Do you want a drink? Gin? Tonic? Fine. I'll just have an orange juice. I don't drink. Got to be careful. You never know who's watching. They're everywhere. Sorry, forget I said that. Even a joke can be paranoia. Do you like my hair? That's a golden gloss rinse. Not my style really: I have this scar down my cheek: see, if I turn to the light? A good short crop is what suits me best, always has been: I suppose I've got what you'd call a strong face. Oops, sorry, dear, didn't mean to spill your gin; it's the heels. I do my best but I can never quite manage stilettos. But it's an ill wind; anyone watching would think I'm ever so slightly tipsy, and that's normal, isn't it. It is not absolutely A-okay not to drink alcohol. On the obsessive side. *Darling, of course there are people watching.*

Let me tell you about the clinical disco while Eddie finishes his game of darts. He hates darts but darts are what men do in pubs, okay? The clinical disco is what they have once a month at Broadmoor. (Yes, that place. Broadmoor. The secure hospital for the criminally insane.) You didn't know they had women there? They do. One woman to every nine men. They often don't look all that like women when they go in but they sure as hell look like them when (and if, if, if, if, if, if) they go out.

How did I get to be in there? You really want to know? I'd been having this crummy time at home and this crummy time at work. I was pregnant and married to this guy I loved, God knows why, in retrospect, but I did, only he fancied my mother, and he got her pregnant too – while I was out at work – did you know women can get pregnant at fifty? He didn't, she didn't, I didn't – but she was! My mum said he only married me to be near her anyway and I was the one who ought to have an abortion. So I did. It went wrong and messed me up inside, so I couldn't have babies, and my mum said what did it matter, I was a lesbian anyway, just look at me. I got the scar in a road accident, in case you're wondering. And I thought what the hell, who wants a man, who wants a mother, and walked out on them. And I was working at the Royal Opera House for this man who was a real pain, and you know how these places get: the dramas and the rows and the overwork and the underpay and the show must go on though you're dropping dead. Dropping dead babies. No, I'm not crying. What do you think I am, a depressive? I'm as normal as the next person.

What I did was set fire to the office. Just an impulse. I was having these terrible pains and he made me work late. He said it was my fault *Der Rosenkavalier's* wig didn't fit: he said I'd made his opera house a laughing stock: the wig slipped and the *New York Times* noticed and jeered. But it wasn't my fault about the wig: wardrobe had put the message through to props, not administration. And I sat in front of the VDU – the union is against them: they cause infertility in women but what employer's going to worry about a thing like that – they'd prefer everyone childless any day – and thought about my husband and my mum, five months pregnant, and lit a cigarette. I'd given up smoking for a whole year but this business at home had made me start again. Have you ever had an abortion at five months? No? Not many have.

How's your drink? How's Eddie getting on with the darts? Started another game? That's A-okay, that's fine by me, that's normal.

So what were we saying, Linda? Oh yes, arson. That's what they called it. I just moved my cigarette lighter under the curtains and they went up, whoosh, and they caught some kind of soundproof ceiling infill they use these days instead of plaster. Up it all went. Whoosh again. Four hundred pounds' worth of da-mage. Or so they said. If you ask me, they were glad of the excuse to redecorate.

Like a fool, instead of lying and just saying it was an accident, I said I'd done it on purpose, I was glad I had,

opera was a waste of public funds, and working late a
waste of my life. That was before I got to court. The
solicitor laddie warned me off. He said arson was no
laughing matter, they came down very hard on arson. I
thought a fine, perhaps: he said no, prison. Years not
months.

You know my mum didn't even come to the
hearing? She had a baby girl. I thought there might
be something wrong with it, my mum being so old, but
there wasn't. Perhaps the father being so young made
up for it.

There was a barrister chappie. He said look you've
been upset, you are upset, all this business at home. The
thing for you to do is plead insane; we'll get you sent to
Broadmoor, it's the best place in the country for
psychiatric care, they'll have you right in the head
in no time. Otherwise it's Holloway, and that's all strip
cells and major tranquillizers, and not so much of a
short sharp shock as a long sharp shock. Years, it could
be, arson.

So that's what I did, I pleaded insane, and got an
indefinite sentence, which meant into Broadmoor
until such time as I was cured and safe to be let out
into the world again. I never was unsafe. You know
what one of those famous opera singers said when
she heard what I'd done? 'Good for Philly,' she said.
'Best thing that could possibly happen: the whole
place razed to the ground.' Only of course it wasn't
razed to the ground, there was just one room already
in need of redecoration slightly blackened. When did
I realize I'd made a mistake? The minute I saw

Broadmoor: a great black pile: the second I got into this reception room. There were three women nurses in there, standing around a bath of hot water; great hefty women, and male nurses too, and they were talking and laughing. Well, not exactly laughing, but an Inside equivalent; a sort of heavy grunting ha-ha-ha they manage, halfway between sex and hate. They didn't even look at me as I came in. I was terrified, you can imagine. One of them said 'strip' over her shoulder and I just stood there not believing it. So she barked 'strip' again, so I took off a cardigan and my shoes, and then one of them just ripped everything off me and pushed my legs apart and yanked out a Tampax – sorry about this, Linda – and threw it in a bin and dunked me in the bath without even seeing me. Do you know what's worse than being naked and seen by strangers, including men strangers? It's being naked and unseen, because you don't even count as a woman. Why men? In case the women patients are uncontrollable. The bath was dirty. So were the nurses. I asked for a sanitary towel but no one replied. I don't know if they were being cruel: I don't think they thought that what came out of my mouth were words. Well I was mad, wasn't I? That's why I was there. I was mad because I was a patient, I was wicked because I was a prisoner: they were sane because they were nurses and good because they could go home after work.

Linda, is that guy over there in the suit watching? No? You're sure?

They didn't go far, mind you, most of them. They lived, breathed, slept The Hospital. Whole families of nurses live in houses at the foot of the great Broadmoor wall. They intermarry. Complain about one and you find you're talking to the cousin, aunt, lover or best friend of the complainee. You learn to shut up: you learn to smile. I was a tea bag for the whole of one day and I never stopped smiling from dawn to dusk. That's right, I was a tea bag. Nurse Kelly put a wooden frame round my shoulders and hung a piece of gauze front and back and said 'You be a tea bag all day' so I was. How we all laughed. Why did he want me to be a tea bag? It was his little joke. They get bored, you see. They look to the patients for entertainment.

Treatment? Linda, I saw one psychiatrist six times and I was there three years. The men do better. They have rehabilitation programmes, ping-pong, carpentry and we all get videos. Only the men get to choose the video and they always choose blue films. They have to choose them to show they're normal, and the women have to choose not to see them to show the same. You have to be normal to get out. Sister in the ward fills in the report cards. She's the one who decides whether or not you're sane enough to go before the Parole Committee. The trouble is, she's not so sane herself. She's more institutionalized than the patients.

Eddie, come and join us! How was your game? You won? Better not do that too often. You don't want to be seen as an over-achiever. This is Linda,

I'm telling her how we met. At the clinical disco. Shall we do a little dance, just the pair of us, in the middle of everything and everyone, just to celebrate being out? No, you're right, that would be just plain mad. Eddie and I love each other, Linda, we met at the clinical disco, down Broadmoor way. Who knows, the doctor may have been wrong about me not having babies; stranger things happen. My mum ran out on my ex, leaving him to look after the baby: he came to visit me in Broadmoor once and asked me to go back to him, but I wouldn't. Sister put me back for that: a proper woman wants to go back to her husband, even though he's her little sister's father. And after he'd gone I cried. You must never cry in Broadmoor. It means you're depressed; and that's the worst madness of all. The staff all love it in there, and think you're really crazy if you don't. I guess they get kind of offended if you cry. So it's on with the lipstick and smile, smile, smile, though everyone around you is ballooning with largactyl and barking like the dogs they think they are.

I tell you something, Linda, these places are madhouses. Never, never plead the balance of your mind is disturbed in court: get a prison sentence and relax, and wait for time to pass and one day you'll be free. Once you're in a secure hospital, you may never get out at all, and they fill the women up with so many tranquillizers, you may never be fit to. The drugs give you brain damage. But I reckon I'm all right; my hands tremble a bit, and my mouth twitches sometimes, but it's not too bad. And I'm still *me*, aren't I.

Eddie's fine – they don't give men so much, sometimes none at all. Only you never know what's in the
tea. But you can't be seen not drinking it, because
that's paranoia.

Eddie says I should sue the barrister, with his fine talk
of therapy and treatment in Broadmoor, but I reckon I
won't. Once you've been in you're never safe. They
can pop you back inside if you cause any trouble at all,
and they're the ones who decide what trouble is. So we
keep our mouths shut and our noses clean, we ex-
inmates of Broadmoor.

Are you sure that man's not watching? Is there
something wrong with us? Eddie? You're not wearing
your earring, are you? Turn your head. No, that's all
right. We look just like everyone else. Don't we? Is my
lipstick smudged? Christ, I hate wearing it. It makes my
eyes look small.

At the clinical disco! They hold them at Broadmoor every month. Lots of the men in there are sex
offenders, rapists, mass murderers, torturers, child
abusers, flashers. The staff like to see how they're
getting on, how they react to the opposite sex, and
on the morning of the disco Sister turns up and says
'you go' and 'you' and 'you' and of course you can't
say no, no matter how scared you are. Because
you're supposed to want to dance. And the male
staff gee up the men – hey, look at those titties!
Wouldn't you like to look up *that* skirt – and stand
by looking forward to the trouble, a bit of living
porno, better than a blue film any day. And they gee
up the women too: wow, there's a handsome hunk

of male: and you have to act interested, because that's normal: if they think you're a lezzie you never get out. And the men have to act interested, but not too interested. Eddie and I met at the clinical disco, acting just gently interested. Eddie felt up my titties, and I rubbed myself against him and the staff watched and all of a sudden he said 'Hey, I mean really,' and I said 'Hi,' and he said 'Sorry about this, keep smiling,' and I said, 'Ditto, what are you in for?' and he said 'I got a job as a woman teacher. Six little girls framed me. But I love teaching, not little girls. There was just no job for a man,' and I believed him: nobody else ever had. And I told him about my mum and my ex, and he seemed to understand. Didn't you, Eddie! That's love, you see. Love at first sight. You're just on the other person's side, and if you can find someone else like that about you, everything falls into place. We were both out in three months. It didn't matter for once if I wore lipstick, it didn't matter to him if he had to watch blue films: you stop thinking that acting sane is driving you mad: you don't have not to cry because you stop wanting to cry: the barking and howling and screeching stop worrying you; I guess when you're in love you're just happy so they have to turn you out; because your being happy shows them up. If you're happy, what does sane or insane mean, what are their lives all about? They can't bear to see it.

Linda, it's been great meeting you. Eddie and I are off home now. I've talked too much. Sorry. When we're our side of our front door I scrub off the make-up and get into jeans and he gets into drag, and we're ourselves, and we just hope no one comes knocking on the door to say, hey that's not normal, back to Broadmoor, but I reckon love's a talisman. If we hold on to that we'll be okay.

1985

The Day the World Came to Somerset

'You can tell the children by the mothers,' said Miss Walters. 'Show me a tidy mother; I'll show you a tidy child.' She spoke definitely. She always did. She knew what the world was like.

'Or the mothers by the children,' said Mrs Windsor, unexpectedly. But she was only an auxiliary; the staff room didn't take much notice of her. She was paid next to nothing. She came in from outside to hear reading, or help in the Infants Class, clearing up accidents or tying shoelaces. 'What I mean is, if I see a child who is happy and easy and bright, I know that child will have a kind mother.' But then, as Miss Jakes, who taught Class 4 and came from London, had remarked (in the new educational patois they all hated), Mrs Windsor was nothing if not child-centred. Soppy, that is.

East Bradley Junior was just about the smallest school in Somerset; threats of closure rumbled like thunder round its ears, and perhaps it was the noise of that thunder which deafened Mr Rossiter, the Headmaster, to the murmured protests of children and staff as he stalked the corridors, tall, grey,

stooping, shouting and snapping at the children
(and usually the wrong children), demanding
peace, quiet and order in classrooms, school hall,
staff room, everywhere; putting this out of bounds,
declaring that out of order, putting pupils in corners
for wearing red socks, disallowing trainers, and even
standing infant wrongdoers in the wastepaper basket
to prove just how worthless their chatter was. The
two dinner ladies had caught his manner. Children
who did not eat up were made to eat up, which kept
Mrs Windsor busy cleaning up pupils who had been
unexpectedly and distressingly sick. Mr Rossiter
hated the PTA, but had to have one. The PTA
raised money and the school was short of money.
Without the parents, the school secretary would have
had no typewriter, let alone paper for the endless
notes, messages and reproaches which streamed out
of the school to the parental world. Mr Rossiter had
liked the old days, when a line had been painted on
the school playground and a notice above it said 'No
Parents Beyond This Point'; even though the LEA's
policy had obliged him to remove these in the mid-
sixties, it was the mid-seventies before the parents
had ventured over the non-existent line. But now
there seemed no keeping them out. The new-style
parents – mostly the ones down from London –
would be in the classrooms before school, after
school, chatting to teachers and pupils, even pop-
ping their heads round doors while lessons were in
progress, with messages about aunties or swimsuits or
lost packed lunches. Lots of pupils took packed

lunches. Mr Rossiter didn't like that. It somehow loosened the school's grip upon the child. It smacked of change: change smacked of chaos.

The names on the school register changed, as the community outside changed. The ordinary Alans and Lindas and Michaels and Annes were sprinkled with Saffrons and Ishtars, Sebs and Felixes. The old stone villages were infilled with bungalows and housing estates: the farm cottages no longer housed farm workers – they'd been replaced long ago by tractors and the machinery of intensive farming – and who had to live on the spot any more? – but had been bought up by wealthy incomers from the cities, or let by farmers to hippy-style households – a safe enough thing to do, because the DHSS paid the rent – and in the meantime house prices went up, and up, and up – but who could blame the farmers? They had to survive somehow: no one wanted them to produce food any more. There was more than enough in the world, it seemed – all those people starved in undeveloped countries not for lack of food but because of someone else's duty to make a profit or be politically in the right. The waves washed right back to East Bradley's door, and changed the names on the school roll.

And the parents seemed to divide these days into the rich and the poor. New Volvos drove up to the school gates while from the school bus limped children who were wearing someone else's shoes, because the parents couldn't afford new; and the school fund was depleted paying the transport fares of children whose parents had to pay but wouldn't, and there were two small children who walked almost six miles every day on their own along an arterial road – little Ellen Bryce and Kelly Rice – and slept or wept all day in lessons. They were both from one-parent families: one mother out to work, the other in need of psychiatric help – or so Miss Jakes said. Miss Walters said Mrs Rice should pull herself together.

It was just about the prettiest school in Somerset: a low stone building next to a twelfth-century church, surrounded by fields: and there was an old oak in the playground, towering above the churchyard yews, which was reputed to be seven hundred years old. Ishtar and Seb, Saffron and Felix played tag around it, along with Alan and Linda, Michael and Anne, and little Cleopatra, too, black as night. When she was older the boys wouldn't go out with her, everyone knew. Though girls, later on, would vie to go out with her big brother Joseph. Okay, even stylish, for a girl to be seen with a black boy: all wrong for a boy to be seen with a black girl. Cleo got called names sometimes – nigger or black bitch – but Joseph didn't. But then Cleo was a tearful, meek little thing, and everyone liked Joseph, who was big, confident and good at football.

Miss Jakes talked about the problems of racism, which was seen in the staff room as absurd, and Miss Walters, whose brother was a police sergeant in Bristol, said the minorities had only themselves to blame, there was bound to be trouble: not quite 'why don't they go back to where they came from', but almost. There was an extraordinary occasion when a Mrs Havelock, a single parent who had come down

from London and made a nuisance of herself on the
PTA, and wore jeans and had fuzzy hair, demanded
that Urdu be taught as a second language, as it was in
Camden. Urdu, taught in London? Compulsory? The
world was going mad. The world would have to be
kept away from East Bradley, Mr Rossiter was the
more determined, and the PTA must be allowed to
talk, but not to act: let it confine itself to making
money. Urdu!

Anyway, the day Mrs Windsor said you could tell
the mothers by the children, the world came right up
to East Bradley Junior School's door, and nothing
was ever the same again. It came in the form of the
Zambezi Boys: a band: a world-famous band, not
quite rock, not quite reggae, all the way from
Zimbabwe, once Rhodesia. A big yellow van, with
'Zambezi Boys' written on it, and some notes of
music and a palm tree or two, stopped outside the
school one Friday afternoon when the children were
rehearsing their end-of-year concert. The driver, a
small black man wearing dark shiny glasses, hopped
out and asked Miss Jakes for directions. They were
on their way to Taunton; they had taken a short cut:
now they were lost. Miss Jakes pointed the way. The
sound of Class 3's 'I am a Snowdrop' drifted through
the open windows. Back got the driver into the van.
The van would not start. Various members of the
band – there were six of them, their leader a massive
young man in a yellow gown even brighter than the
van – got out, kicked it, or fiddled with the engine,
or stood around discussing the matter – just like

anyone else, as Miss Walters later remarked – and
then asked to come in to call the AA. (Rebecca
Ruddle, the AA man's daughter, was in 6A, and the
only child in the school ever to have been in trouble
with the police.) Which they did, from the school
office. And then of course they had to wait for
Rebecca Ruddle's dad. And the sensible place to
wait was lined up against the back wall of the school
hall while 2A sang, and the head boy, Harry Young,
tentatively turned up the sound equipment – borrowed from Currys, whose daughter Melanie was in
3B – to make their tiny, timorous voices carry – and
the children stopped paying attention to 2A's 'All
Things Bright and Beautiful' and turned their heads
to see these extraordinary, brilliantly gowned men
(men in dresses) who all of a sudden were standing
there. And then – no one quite knew how it
happened, though afterwards someone said it was
Mrs Windsor of all people who set it in motion – the
Zambezi Boys were carrying their instruments in and
setting them up, and giving a performance to the
children and staff of East Bradley School. They, who
could fill Wembley, not to mention Bristol's Colston
Hall, they for whom the young of the world yearned
and would empty their pockets (and other people's as
well, no doubt, the way the world is now), played for
the children of East Bradley School! And when the
parents arrived, because when the time came to
collect the children the Zambezi Boys were still
playing, they got out of their Volvos and 2CVs
and Austin Travellers, leaving them parked any old

how, and peered through the windows, and the villagers did the same, because the beat was so loud and strong and extraordinary it had brought them all out of their houses. For Harry Young, usually bright and clean and tidy and responsible, got so carried away that he turned the sound system up, up, up, right up (and those drums and the synthesizer – or was it an African piano? – were loud, very loud, even by themselves). The crows rose and cawed for miles around, the heads of the sheep turned, and cows paused in their grazing, as the beat of Africa, so different from Somerset's slow, heavy heartbeat, escaped out of East Bradley School's hall. Look, Mr Rossiter was furious! But what could he do?

One (slow), two (slow), three-four-five (quick), the beat went, simple but not simple, somehow interlaced and interwoven. The children tapped their feet: the children shook their shoulders: the children looked at their teachers: their teachers were tapping too (but who could help it?) and then all were clapping, because the man in the yellow gown up on the platform was clapping his hands above his head – one, two, three-four-five – faster, faster, faster, now they were clapping on their own, and he was singing, what was it about? Sometimes in a strange language, sometimes in English, about brotherhood, freedom, jubilation, exultation – and Mrs Windsor was on her feet – dancing, Mrs Windsor! Which of the children was the first to move? Why, all agreed later it was little Kelly Rice who didn't have much to lose, who just didn't seem to care about Mr Rossiter – anyway, one of them was on her feet, jigging about, dancing, and then all the children followed, out of their seats, dancing, clapping, laughing – one, two, three-four-five – and the band roared its approval, and the great firm drumbeats and the laughing crash of the hi-hat got into the bloodstream, and Miss Walters (ever prudent) actually pushed chairs out of the way so no one hurt themselves, and took off her tight shoes to dance the better, and Miss Jakes just gave up and laughed and danced herself silly, and the parents stopped peering in at the windows and came in without so much as a by-your-leave and joined in, including Mrs – or what did she call herself? – Ms Havelock (even that seemed okay; let everyone do what they wanted: perhaps these singing, leaping men were speaking Urdu, in which case every word and not every tenth word they chanted or sang made sense), and Darren Gorren, the bus driver no one liked because he'd have no talking on his bus (not even whispering), came in and smiled and caught Miss Robinson of 4B by the hand and danced with her, and amongst the children friends danced with enemies, and enemies with friends, and the retired General Godden who put stones up on his patch of green to stop the parents clipping it with their tyres actually hopped about as best he could and his single strand of long white hair rose and fell to the beat; and look, on every fourth beat the man in the yellow gown leapt into the air, higher, higher, was it possible? He seemed held in the air, actually poised in

the sheer energy of the music and the dance, somewhere near the ceiling, suspended by the animation
and will of the Somerset children, old-style, new-
style – up, up, stay-stay-stay – and as he stayed the
church bell actually rang – dong, dong, just twice, on
the beat – the vicar later said it must have been the
vibration (thank you, Currys, for your technological
assistance, thank you, Harry Young, for your act of
grace, thank you, Zambezi Boys, for your wonderful
performance) – and then Rebecca Ruddle's father
the AA man finally turned up, and wondered what
was going on, was everyone mad, and saw his
daughter dancing and laughing and for some reason
the shame of her disgrace was washed away (she'd
broken into a Taunton pub with a group of older
boys and stolen some cigarettes and had had to
appear in the Juvenile Court), and he felt more
cheerful than he had for months, and when he tried
the Zambezi Boys' van the motor simply started –
why it hadn't before he couldn't make out.

And as the engine started, the music stopped. The
dancing, the cheering, the stamping died. And then
little Ishtar Heddle flung herself against the door, arms
outstretched. 'Don't go,' she cried. 'More! More!'
'More, more,' commanded the children, roaring and
stamping – how could such little things make such a
noise? – and the Zambezi Boys obeyed. The great
obeyed the little. The beat began again, as if it had
merely been waiting for the order: the guitar
thrummed, the synthesizer sang, and down from the
platform leapt the man in the yellow gown and grabbed

poor flustered helpless Mr Rossiter by the hands and made him dance – made Mr Rossiter dance! – and dance he did, and as he danced his arthritis, or whatever it was that made his limbs so stiff, seemed to fall away, and Mr Rossiter smiled and stopped counting the children who wore trainers and planning his individual letters to parents – because didn't trainers make less noice than the clump, clump, clump-clump-clump of the properly black-booted children? – and he beamed at the staff, and he beamed at the children, and even at the parents, even at Ms Havelock, who was, even as she danced, quite startled. Then, as suddenly as it began, it stopped.

'Peace, exultation, jubilation', cried the young man in the yellow gown who could be sustained in mid-air by the energy of his being, 'to the brotherhood of man!'

'And the sisterhood!' cried Ms Havelock. 'Don't forget the sisterhood.' And they were gone. The Zambezi Boys were gone.

And after that nothing was quite the same, if only that Scott Hockney in Infants never dirtied his pants again – perhaps a miracle, or just because he'd jigged about so much he got some kind of control over his muscles – so the other children would play with him (and Mrs Windsor reported he could remember that the mysterious t-h-e spelt the extraordinary 'the' from the next Monday right through to the next Friday and for ever thereafter). And Ms Havelock took to going miles out of her way each day to take and fetch Kelly and Ellen in her 2CV instead of saying that to do so was system-bolstering and a child or two would have to die before the under-three-mile-no-free-transport system was reformed. And Neal Hodder's Dad, who'd also danced, decided on the whole he'd better not crop-spray the field behind the school in spite of the stuff's being officially specified safe; and everyone wore trainers ever after, they being so much better for dancing, and no one kept their Kit-Kats and crisps to themselves at break, as had lately been their habit (for the greed and self-interest of governments is as catching as measles), but began to share them with the limping children off the bus, who no longer limped because trainers can be cheap and interchangeable – was not this the brotherhood, not to mention the sisterhood, of man, not to mention woman? And the dinner ladies cooked a little better and with more charity, so the children ate up better; and at the first sign of trouble there'd be a kind of thrumming of fingers on desks – one, two, three-four-five – and the trouble evaporated; and if Mr Rossiter felt his anxiety and irritation returning, and began to express it, there'd be a kind of dancing note thrumming on the floor as the children fell into step – one, two, three-four-five – on the stairs and down the corridors, and he'd hold his tongue, and just nod, and smile, and not a word had to be said; and little Cleo put her hand in Miss Walters', who let it stay there, and even put her up for the Class Achievement Award, and the waste-paper basket in the Infants somehow got lost and was never found again. One, two, three-four-five.

Nothing was ever the same again after the Zambezi Boys came to East Bradley by mistake, on their way to Taunton, and brought with them in their yellow van the good things of the wider world – exultation, jubilation, joy, the throb of the universe – and in their easy generosity passed them on. Such things happen. That was the day the world came to Somerset, and couldn't be kept out.

1989

Un Crime Maternel

What did they call you? Miss Jacobs? I find that very strange. Only a mother, surely, can understand a mother. What is their purpose in having me see you? If anyone is crazy, it's the law, not me. If it asks for psychiatric reports, which frankly I see as both demeaning to me and damaging to my children, it might at least find someone competent to do the reporting. Or do they have to scrape the barrel for people such as yourself? I don't suppose it's a barrel of laughs, coming here to Holloway and sitting in this horrid little airless green room smelling of cabbage with a locked door and not even a window. In fact the room is rather like the inside of my head used to be before I battered my way out of it, made a hole to let in the air and the light.

Fortunately I can wear my own clothes, being on remand; I don't have to wear their nasty dingy dresses. There isn't an iron available but I keep my skirt beneath my mattress overnight, so the pleats stay in. I like to be smart. I am in the habit of being smart. It's so important to set an example to the children, don't you think? But I suppose you wouldn't know.

Now listen, Miss Jacobs, I will have to make do with you since you're all I have to work with. It is absolutely imperative, do you understand, that you declare me of sound mind. It would do Janet and Harvey no good at all to believe that their mother was insane. It would be too big a burden for them to bear. They are already having to cope with the loss of their father, and Janet's birthday is tomorrow – she will be eight – and she will be disturbed enough that for the first birthday ever when she wakes I'm not there by her bed to say 'Happy birthday, darling.' She may begin to worry, or doubt what she's been told; which is, very sensibly, that I'm on holiday in Greece getting over Peter's death and will be back soon. When I'm out of here I'll be able to talk the whole thing through with the pair of them. It's so important to tell children the truth: if you do, their trust in you is never diminished. Time passes so slowly for children: it is vital that I get back to them as soon as possible: that all this silly and unnecessary fuss comes to an immediate end. They're with Peter's parents, and though Graham and Jenny are not quite as child-centred as I'd like them to be, for people of that generation they're not bad. I can be confident they'll have the sense not to let Janet see the newspapers and of course Harvey isn't reading yet. I used to worry about Harvey's slowness at letters – Janet read at four, and he's already six – but I admit it has its advantages, however unexpected. Crime maternel must be recognized in this country, as crime passionnel is in

France. To kill for one's children is no crime: rather, it is something for which a mother should be honoured. I want a medal, Miss Jacobs, not to be had up on a murder charge and remanded without bail for psychiatric reports. I did what it was my duty to do. I chose my children's interests over my husband's interests. Their lives, after all, were just beginning. We do give children this precedence as a matter of course.

It is imperative that I stand trial as a sane person and am properly acquitted, Miss Jacobs, because then the children can deal with it. It may mean moving house and changing schools and names afterwards, of course, but that is nothing compared to the avoidance of trauma. You must see, Miss Jacobs, that I did the only thing I could, in the circumstances I was in.

I had a troubled childhood myself. A father who molested me, a mother who let it happen. I was fostered when I was twelve by a very kind and pleasant family. I know there is good as well as bad in the world. I always wanted to have children, and to give them a perfect life. What is there more important in the world than this? I became a nurse and did well in my profession, but always with my future role as a mother in mind. I am not bad looking, and could, and indeed would, have married on several occasions, but each time I felt the man involved would not make a good enough father. He would have to be loving, kind, genial, patient, intelligent, sensitive to children's needs, and able to provide the proper male authority role within the family group. I began to think I'd never meet the perfect father. I could settle, even happily, for less than perfection for myself, but not for my unborn children!

And finally I met him! Peter! He fulfilled all my requirements, as I did his. He looked for the perfect mother, as I looked for the perfect father. We married, and agreed we would wait a year before starting a family so the children would be born into a settled and secure domestic framework. And that year, I may say, was exceedingly happy. I had always felt, because of my early experience, that sex was not for me. That year with Peter proved me wrong! Then, according to plan, I became pregnant with Janet, and of course after she was born sex became impossible. She could only sleep if she was in the bed with us, and then only if she was at the breast, and I got an ulcer, and you know how it is with small babies. Well, you don't, do you. Let me just say Janet was a sensitive baby, and cried a lot, and then when Harvey came along he turned out to be hyperactive, and I'm sorry to say Peter's views on child-rearing began to change: they simply did not coincide any more with mine.

Does this sound like the tale of a mad woman? I promise you I am not mad.

Peter was teaching at the time, and spent far too much time away from home. I know he had obligations to pupils and college, but he had obligations to his children as well. I insisted that he always be home by bathtime. It is imperative that children have the reassurance that a rock-solid routine provides. But sometimes, on some spurious ground or other, he would be absent. I would have to watch their little faces fall. Splashing about in the water, so important to the development of their tactile responses, their creative drive, just wasn't the same without Daddy. And so he and I began to quarrel. The atmosphere in the home became tense, and that's so very bad for children. They pick up really quickly on vibes.

Peter could, and would, sometimes even in front of them, say terrible things to me. 'Why do you always ask those children questions?' he'd yell. 'Why do you say, "Are you sleepy? Would you like to go in your cot?" Why don't you say, "You do feel sleepy, darling. Now I'm putting you in your cot"?' And of course the answer was so obvious! For one thing, children are not there for the parents' convenience, to be shut up; for another, even with the smallest child it is important to develop consciousness of self. The child knows what it feels; it is up to the parent to decipher those feelings and act upon them. I don't *tell* my child it is hungry: I require it to give me an accurate account of what's going on in its head. That way it learns self-expression. How else? Peter would accuse me of unforgivable things – of over-stimulating the children, of depriving them of pleasure – by which he only meant he'd shut them up if he could by shoving ice lollies in their mouths which would rot their teeth and give them a liking for sweet things which might stay with them all their lives, for all he knew. Or, I'm sorry to say, cared. Please don't think he was a bad father, he wasn't. He loved Janet and Harvey immoderately, and they loved him, which was of course the trouble. I'd feel like tucking them under my arm and running off with them, but how could I? Within two minutes they'd be grizzling and pining for their father.

The upshot of our disagreements over child-care, together with the actuality of those two small lively children, meant I was easily riled and distressed, and spent quite a lot of time in tears which I could not control. Try as I would to be brave and bright for the children's sake, I failed. They would see me red-eyed and depressed, and hear Peter shouting. It couldn't go on. It is the most traumatic and damaging thing for children to hear their parents rowing. Unforgivable to let it happen but it was not my doing. It began to look as if we had to part. Between us we had to provide two loving and caring environments between which Harvey and Janet would travel, since we could not make one. Now I knew I would do my part in this. But I was not convinced he would do his. Already Peter was seeing another woman, a junkfood addict whose idea of an afternoon out with the children was to go to McDonald's on the way to the zoo – can you imagine, a *zoo*? – the torment of those poor wild caged creatures – and Janet and Harvey actively encouraged to gawp and throw peanuts. Now I'm well aware that it's best for children to see their parents happy, and Peter's sex drive was such that he could only be happy if it was more or less satisfied. I had no grudge whatsoever against his girlfriends, one or all of them, so don't be misled by anyone who says mine was a crime passionnel. It was most definitely – if crime it was – a crime maternel. An act committed for the sake of the children which involves the death and/or disenabling of an incompetent and/or damaging parent. It wasn't Peter's *fault* that this was what he was. Blame God, if you must blame anyone, for creating parents and children whose emotional interests overlap but do not coincide. But there it was. I could see no other way out of an impossible bind.

Divorce, when it comes to it, is so crippling to the child's psyche, is it not? The children suffer appallingly when a family breaks up. Statistics show that a paternal death has a less damaging effect on the children than divorce, so long as the family home is maintained and family income does not fall. So what else could I do, Miss Jacobs? In my children's interests?

I insured Peter's life and he and I, his girlfriend and the children went for a country walk and we picked mushrooms, including a death cap, and I made a beef casserole that evening, and he and she ate it – I am a vegetarian and I never let the children eat beef because of the possibility of mad cow disease but Peter of course would never renounce beef: what he liked he had to have – and it proved as fatal as the books said. Don't worry – I got the pair of them into hospital promptly so the children witnessed nothing nasty. I hadn't realized how suspicious coroners and police can be – I suppose I do tend to think everyone is as child-centred as I am. But this is not insanity, Miss Jacobs, is it? I was doing my best for my children, as the statistics in our society suggest the best to be: and I must get back to them as soon as is humanly possible, for their sake. I presume the court won't be so stupid as not to understand that? What do you think?

1990

Alopecia

It's 1972.

'Fiddlesticks,' says Maureen. Everyone else says 'crap' or 'balls', but Maureen's current gear, being Victorian sprigged muslin, demands an appropriate vocabulary. 'Fiddlesticks. If Erica says her bald patches are anything to do with Derek, she's lying. It's alopecia.'

'I wonder which would be worse,' murmurs Ruthie in her soft voice, 'to have a husband who tears your hair out in the night, or to have alopecia.'

Ruthie wears a black fringed satin dress exactly half a century old, through which, alas, Ruthie's ribs show even more prominently than her breasts. Ruthie's little girl Poppy (at four too old for playgroup, too young for school), wears a long, white (well, yellowish) cotton shift which contrasts nicely with her mother's dusty black.

'At least the husband might improve, with effort,' says Alison, 'unlike alopecia. You wake up one morning with a single bald patch and a month or so later there you are, completely bald. Nothing anyone

can do about it.' Alison, plump mother of three,
sensibly wears a flowered Laura Ashley dress which
hides her bulges.

'It might be quite interesting,' remarks Maureen.
'The egg-head approach. One would have to forgo the
past, of course, and go all space-age, which would
hardly be in keeping with the mood of the times.'

'You are the mood of the times, Maureen,' murmurs
Ruthie, as expected. Ruthie's simple adulation of
Maureen is both gratifying and embarrassing, every-
one agrees.

Everyone agrees, on the other hand, that Erica
Bisham of the bald patches is a stupid, if ladylike, bitch.

Maureen, Ruthie and Alison are working in Maureen's premises off the Kings Road. Here Maureen, as
befits the glamour of her station, the initiator of
Mauromania, meets the media, expresses opinions,
answers the phone, dictates to secretaries (male),
selects and matches fabrics, approves designs and
makes, in general, multitudinous decisions – although
not, perhaps, as multitudinous as the ones she was
accustomed to make in the middle and late sixties,
when the world was young and rich and wild. Maureen
is forty but you'd never think it. She wears a large hat
by day (and, one imagines, night) which shades her
anxious face and guards her still pretty complexion.
Maureen leads a rich life. Maureen once had her pubic
hair dyed green to match her fingernails – or so her
husband Kim announced to a waiting (well, such were
the days) world: she divorced him not long after,
having lost his baby at five months. The head of the

foetus, rumour had it, emerged green, and her National Health Service GP refused to treat her any more, and she had to go private after all – she with her Marxist convictions.

That was 1968. If the state's going to tumble, let it tumble. The sooner the better. Drop out, everyone! Mauromania magnifique! And off goes Maureen's husband Kim with Maureen's au pair – a broad-hipped, big-bosomed girl, good breeding material, with an ordinary coarse and curly brush, if somewhat reddish.

Still, it had been a good marriage as marriages go. And as marriages go, it went. Or so Maureen remarked to the press, on her way home (six beds, six baths, four recep., American kitchen, patio, South Ken) from the divorce courts. Maureen cried a little in the taxi, when she'd left her public well behind, partly from shock and grief, mostly from confusion that beloved Kim, Kim, who so despised the nuclear family, who had so often said that he and she ought to get divorced in order to have a true and unfettered relationship, that Maureen's Kim should have speeded up Maureen's divorce in order to marry Maureen's au pair girl before the baby arrived. Kim and Maureen had been married for fifteen years. Kim had been Kevin from Liverpool before seeing the light or at any rate the guru. Maureen had always been just Maureen from Hoxton, East London: remained so through the birth, rise and triumph of Mauromania. It was her charm. Local girl makes good.

Maureen has experience of life: she knows by now, having also been married to a psychiatrist who ran off with all her money and the marital home, that it is wise to watch what people do, not listen to what they say. Well, it's something to have learned. Ruthie and Alison, her (nominal) partners from the beginning, each her junior by some ten years, listen to Maureen with respect and diffidence.

'Mind you,' says Maureen now, matching up purple feathers with emerald satin to great effect. 'if I were Derek I'd certainly beat Erica to death. Fancy having to listen to that whining voice night after night. The only trouble is he's become too much of a gentleman. He'll never have the courage to do it. Turned his back on his origins, and all that. It doesn't do.'

Maureen has known Derek since the old days in Hoxton. They were evacuees together: shared the same bomb shelter on their return from Starvation Hall in Felixstowe – a boys' public school considered unsafe for the gentry's children but all right for the East Enders.

'It's all Erica's fantasy,' says Ruthie, knowledgeably. 'A kind of dreadful sexual fantasy. She *wants* him to beat her up so she trots round London saying he does. Poor Derek. It comes from marrying into the English upper classes, old style. She must be nearly fifty. She has that kind of battered-looking face.'

Her voice trails away. There is a slight pause in the conversation.

'Um,' says Alison.

'That's drink,' says Maureen, decisively. 'Poor bloody Derek. What a ball-breaker to have married.' Derek was Maureen's childhood sweetheart. What a romantic, platonic idyll! She nearly married him once, twice, three times. Once in the very early days, before Kim, before anyone, when Derek was selling books from a barrow in Hoxton market. Once again, after Kim and before the professor, by which time Derek was taking expensive photographs of the trendy and successful – only then Erica turned up in Derek's bed, long-legged, disdainful, beautiful, with a model's precise and organised face, and the fluty tones of the girl who'd bought her school uniform at Harrods, and that was the end of that. Not that Derek had ever exactly proposed to Maureen; not that they'd ever even been to bed together: they just knew each other and each other's bed partners so well that each knew what the other was thinking, feeling, hoping. Both from Hoxton, East London: Derek, Maureen; and a host of others, too. What was there, you might ask, about that particular acre of the East End which over a period of a few years gave birth to such a crop of remarkable children, such a flare-up of human creativity in terms of writing, painting, designing, entertaining? Changing the world? One might almost think God had chosen it for an experiment in intensive talent-breeding. Mauromania, God-sent.

And then there was another time in the late sixties, when there was a short break between Derek and Erica – Erica had a hysterectomy against Derek's wishes; but during those two weeks of opportunity Maureen, her business flourishing, her designs world famous, Mauromania a label for even trendy young queens (royal, that is) to boast, rich beyond counting – during those two special weeks of all weeks Maureen fell head over heels classically in love with Pedro: no, not a fisherman, but as good as – Italian, young, open-shirted, sloe-eyed, a designer. And Pedro, it later transpired, was using Maureen as a means to laying all the models, both male and female (Maureen had gone into menswear). Maureen was the last to know, and by the time she did Derek was in Erica's arms (or whatever) again. A sorry episode. Maureen spent six months at a health farm, on a diet of grapes and brown rice. At the end of that time Mauromania Man had collapsed, her business manager had jumped out of a tenth-floor window, and an employee's irate mother was bringing a criminal suit against Maureen personally for running a brothel. It was all quite irrational. If the employee, a runaway girl of, it turned out, only thirteen, but looking twenty, and an excellent seamstress, had contracted gonorrhoea whilst in her employ, was that Maureen's fault? The judge, sensibly, decided it wasn't, and that the entire collapse of British respectability could not fairly be laid at Maureen's door. Legal costs came to more than £12,000; the country house and stables had to be sold at a knock-down price. That was disaster year.

And who was there during that time to hold Maureen's hand? No one. Everyone, it seemed, had troubles enough of their own. And all the time, Maureen's poor heart bled for Pedro, of the ridiculous name and the sloe eyes, long departed, laughing, streptococci surging in his wake. And of all the old friends and allies only Ruthie and Alison lingered on, two familiar faces in a sea of changing ones, getting

younger every day, and hungrier year by year not for
fun, fashion, and excitement, but for money, promotion, security, and acknowledgment.

The staff even went on strike once, walking up and
down outside the workshop with placards announcing
hours and wages, backed by Maoists, women's libera-
tionists and trade unionists, all vying for their trumpery
allegiance, puffing up a tiny news story into a colossal
media joke, not even bothering to get Maureen's side
of the story – absenteeism, drug addiction, shoddy
workmanship, falling markets, constricting profits.

But Ruthie gave birth to Poppy, unexpectedly, in
the black and gold ladies' rest-room (customers only –
just as well it wasn't in the staff toilets where the plaster
was flaking and the old wall-cisterns came down on
your head if you pulled the chain) and that cheered
everyone up. Business perked up, staff calmed down as
unemployment rose. Poppy, born of Mauromania, was
everyone's favourite, everyone's mascot. Her father,
only seventeen, was doing two years inside, framed by
the police for dealing in pot. He did not have too bad a
time – he got three A-levels and university entrance
inside, which he would not have got outside, but it
meant poor little Poppy had to do without a father's
care and Ruthie had to cope on her own. Ruthie of the
ribs.

Alison, meanwhile, somewhat apologetically, had
married Hugo, a rather straight and respectable actor
who believed in women's rights; they had three
children and lived in a cosy house with a garden in
Muswell Hill: Alison even belonged to the PTA! Hugo

was frequently without work, but Hugo and Alison
managed, between them, to keep going and even
happy. Now Hugo thinks Alison should ask for a
rise, but Alison doesn't like to. That's the trouble
about working for a friend and being only a nominal
partner.

'Don't let's talk about Erica Bisham any more,' says
Maureen. 'It's too draggy a subject.' So they don't.

But one midnight a couple of weeks later, when
Maureen, Ruthie and Alison are working late to
meet an order – as is their frequent custom these days
(and one most unnerving to Hugo, Alison's husband)
– there comes a tap on the door. It's Erica, of course.
Who else would tap, in such an ingratiating fashion?
Others cry 'Hi!' or 'Peace!' and enter Erica, smiling
nervously and crookedly; her yellow hair eccentric in
the extreme; bushy in places, sparse in others.
Couldn't she wear a wig? She is wearing a Marks
& Spencer nightie which not even Ruthie would
think of wearing, in the house or out of it. It is
bloodstained down the back. (Menstruation is not yet
so fashionable as to be thus demonstrable, though it
can be talked about at length.) A strong smell of
what? alcohol, or is it nail varnish? hangs about her.
Drinking again. (Alison's husband, Hugo, in a long
period of unemployment, once veered on to the
edge of alcoholism but fortunately veered off again,
and the smell of nail varnish, acetone, gave a warning
sign of an agitated, overworked liver, unable to cope
with acetaldehyde, the highly toxic product of
alcohol metabolism.)

'Could I sit down?' says Erica. 'He's locked me out. Am I speaking oddly? I think I've lost a tooth. I'm hurting under my ribs and I feel sick.'

They stare at her – this drunk, dishevelled, trouble-making woman.

'He,' says Maureen finally. 'Who's he?'

'Derek.'

'You're going to get into trouble, Erica,' says Ruthie, though more kindly than Maureen, 'if you go round saying dreadful things about poor Derek.'

'I wouldn't have come here if there was anywhere else,' says Erica.

'You must have friends,' observes Maureen, as if to say, Don't count us amongst them if you have.

'No.' Erica sounds desolate. 'He has his friends at work. I don't seem to have any.'

'I wonder why,' says Maureen under her breath; and then, 'I'll get you a taxi home, Erica. You're in no state to be out.'

'I'm not drunk, if that's what you think.'

'Who ever is,' sighs Ruthie, sewing relentlessly on. Four more blouses by one o'clock. Then, thank God, bed.

Little Poppy has passed out on a pile of orange ostrich feathers. She looks fantastic.

'If Derek does beat you up,' says Alison, who has seen her father beat her mother on many a Saturday night, 'why don't you go to the police?'

'I did once, and they told me to go home and behave myself.'

'Or leave him?' Alison's mother left Alison's father.

'Where would I go? How would I live? The children? I'm not well.' Erica sways. Alison puts a chair beneath her. Erica sits, legs planted wide apart, head down. A few drops of blood fall on the floor. From Erica's mouth, or elsewhere? Maureen doesn't see, doesn't care. Maureen's on the phone, calling radio cabs who do not reply.

'I try not to provoke him, but I never know what's going to set him off,' mumbles Erica. 'Tonight it was Tampax. He said only whores wore Tampax. He tore it out and kicked me. Look.'

Erica pulls up her nightie (Erica's wearing no knickers) and exposes her private parts in a most shameful, shameless fashion. The inner thighs are blue and mottled, but then, dear God, she's nearly fifty.

What does one look like, thigh-wise, nearing fifty? Maureen's the nearest to knowing, and she's not saying. As for Ruthie, she hopes she'll never get there. Fifty!

'The woman's mad,' mutters Maureen. 'Perhaps I'd better call the loony wagon, not a taxi?'

'Thank God Poppy's asleep.' Poor Ruthie seems in a state of shock.

'You can come home with me, Erica,' says Alison. 'God knows what Hugo will say. He hates matrimonial upsets. He says if you get in between, they both start hitting you.'

Erica gurgles, a kind of mirthless laugh. From behind her, mysteriously, a child steps out. She is eight, stocky, plain and pale, dressed in boring Ladybird pyjamas.

'Mummy?'

Erica's head whips up; the blood on Erica's lip is wiped away by the back of Erica's hand. Erica straightens her back. Erica smiles. Erica's voice is completely normal, ladylike.

'Hallo, darling. How did you get here?'

'I followed you. Daddy was too angry.'

'He'll be better soon, Libby,' says Erica brightly. 'He always is.'

'We're not going home? Please don't let's go home. I don't want to see Daddy.'

'Bitch,' mutters Maureen, 'she's even turned his own child against him. Poor bloody Derek. There's nothing at all the matter with her. Look at her now.'

For Erica is on her feet, smoothing Libby's hair, murmuring, laughing.

'Poor bloody Erica,' observes Alison. It is the first time she has ever defied Maureen, let alone challenged her wisdom. And rising with as much dignity as her plump frame and flounced cotton will allow, Alison takes Erica and Libby home and instals them for the night in the spare room of the cosy house in Muswell Hill.

Hugo isn't any too pleased. 'Your smart sick friends,' he says. And, 'I'd beat a woman like that to death myself, any day.' And, 'Dragging that poor child into it: it's appalling.' He's nice to Libby, though, and rings up Derek to say she's safe and sound, and looks after her while Alison takes Erica round to the doctor. The doctor sends Erica round to the hospital, and the hospital admits her for tests and treatment.

'Why bother?' enquires Hugo. 'Everyone knows she's mad.'

In the evening, Derek comes all the way to Muswell Hill in his Ferrari to pick up Libby. He's an attractive man: intelligent and perspicacious, fatherly and gentle. Just right, it occurs to Alison, for Maureen.

'I'm so sorry about all this,' he says. 'I love my wife dearly but she has her problems. There's a dark side to her nature – you've no idea. A deep inner violence – which of course manifests itself in this kind of behaviour. She's deeply psychophrenic. I'm so afraid for the child.'

'The hospital did admit her,' murmurs Alison. 'And not to the psychiatric ward, but the surgical.'

'That will be her hysterectomy scar again,' says Derek. 'Any slight tussle – she goes quite wild, and I have to restrain her for her own safety – and it opens up. It's symptomatic of her inner sickness, I'm afraid. She even says herself it opens to let the build-up of wickedness out. What I can't forgive is the way she drags poor little Libby into things. She's turning the child against me. God knows what I'm going to do. Well, at least I can bury myself in work. I hear you're an actor, Hugo.'

Hugo offers Derek a drink, and Derek offers (well, more or less) Hugo a part in a new rock musical going on in the West End. Alison goes to visit Erica in hospital.

'Erica has some liver damage, but it's not irreversible: she'll be feeling nauseous for a couple of months, that's all. She's lost a back tooth and she's had a couple of stitches put in her vagina,' says Alison to Maureen and Ruthie next day. The blouse order never got completed – re-orders now look dubious. But if staff haven't the loyalty to work unpaid overtime any more, what else can be expected? The partners (nominal) can't do everything.

'Who said so?' enquires Maureen, sceptically. 'The hospital or Erica?'

'Well,' Alison is obliged to admit, 'Erica.'

'You are an innocent, Alison.' Maureen sounds quite cross. 'Erica can't open her poor sick mouth without uttering a lie. It's her hysterectomy scar opened up again, that's all. No wonder. She's a nymphomaniac: she doesn't leave Derek alone month in, month out. She has the soul of a whore. Poor man. He's so upset by it all. Who wouldn't be?'

Derek takes Maureen out to lunch. In the evening, Alison goes to visit Erica in hospital, but Erica has gone. Sister says, oh yes, her husband came to fetch her. They hadn't wanted to let her go so soon but Mr Bisham seemed such a sensible, loving man, they thought he could look after his wife perfectly well, and it's always nicer at home, isn't it? Was it *the* Derek Bisham? Yes she'd thought so. Poor Mrs Bisham – what a dreadful world we live in, when a respectable married woman can't even walk the streets without being brutally attacked, sexually assaulted by strangers.

It's 1974.

Winter. A chill wind blowing, a colder one still to come. A three-day week imposed by an insane government. Strikes, power cuts, black-outs. Maureen, Ruthie and Alison work by candlelight. All three wear fun-furs – old stock, unsaleable. Poppy is staying with Ruthie's mother, as she usually is these days. Poppy has been developing a squint, and the doctor says she has to wear glasses with one blanked-out lens for at least eighteen months. Ruthie, honestly, can't bear to see her daughter thus. Ruthie's mother, of a prosaic nature, a lady who buys her clothes at C & A Outsize, doesn't seem to mind.

'If oil prices go up,' says Maureen gloomily, 'what's going to happen to the price of synthetics? What's going to happen to Mauromania, come to that?'

'Go up market,' says Alison, 'the rich are always with us.'

Maureen says nothing. Maureen is bad tempered, these days. She is having some kind of painful trouble with her teeth, which she seems less well able to cope with than she can the trouble with staff (overpaid), raw materials (unavailable), delivery dates (impossible), distribution (unchancy), costs (soaring), profits (falling), reinvestment (non-existent). And the snow has ruined the penthouse roof and it has to be replaced, at the cost of many thousands. Men friends come and go: they seem to get younger and less feeling. Sometimes Maureen feels they treat her as a joke. They ask her about the sixties as if it were a different age: of Mauromania as if it were something as dead as the dodo – but it's still surely a label which counts for something, brings in foreign currency, ought really to bring her some recognition. The Beatles got the MBE; why not Maureen of Mauromania? Throw-away clothes for throw-away people?

'Ruthie,' says Maureen. 'You're getting careless. You've put the pocket on upside-down, and it's going for copying. That's going to hold up the whole batch. Oh, what the hell. Let it go through.

'Do you ever hear anything of Erica Bisham?' Ruthie asks Alison, more to annoy Maureen than because she wants to know. 'Is she still wandering round in the middle of the night?'

'Hugo does a lot of work for Derek, these days,' says Alison carefully. 'But he never mentions Erica.'

'Poor Derek. What a fate. A wife with alopecia! I expect she's bald as a coot by now. As good a revenge as any, I dare say.'

'It was nothing to do with alopecia,' says Alison. 'Derek just tore out chunks of her hair, nightly.' Alison's own marriage isn't going so well. Hugo's got the lead in one of Derek's long runs in the West End. Show business consumes his thoughts and ambitions. The ingenue lead is in love with Hugo and says so, on TV quiz games and in the Sunday supplements. She's under age. Alison feels old, bored and boring.

'These days I'd believe anything,' says Ruthie. 'She must provoke him dreadfully.'

'I don't know what you've got against Derek, Alison,' says Maureen. 'Perhaps you just don't like men. In which case you're not much good in a fashion house. Ruthie, that's another pocket upside-down.'

'I feel sick,' says Ruthie. Ruthie's pregnant again. Ruthie's husband was out of prison and with her for exactly two weeks; then he flew off to Istanbul to smuggle marijuana back into the country. He was caught. Now he languishes in a Turkish jail. 'What's to become of us?'

'We must develop a sense of sisterhood,' says Alison, 'that's all.'

Alison's doorbell rings at three in the morning. It is election night, and Alison is watching the results on television. Hugo (presumably) is watching them somewhere else, with the ingenue lead – now above the age of consent, which spoils the pleasure somewhat. It is Erica and Libby. Erica's nose is broken. Libby, at ten, is now in charge. Both are in their nightclothes. Alison pays off the taxi-driver, who won't take a tip. 'What a world,' he says.

'I couldn't think where else to come,' says Libby. 'Where he wouldn't follow her. I wrote down this address last time I was here. I thought it might come in useful, sometime.'

It is the end of Alison's marriage, and the end of Alison's job. Hugo, whose future career largely depends on Derek's goodwill, says, you have Erica in the house or you have me. Alison says, I'll have Erica. 'Lesbian, dyke,' says Hugo, bitterly. 'Don't think you'll keep the children, you won't.'

Maureen says, 'That was the first and last time Derek ever hit her. He told me so. She lurched towards him on purpose. She *wanted* her nose broken; idiot Alison, don't you understand? Erica nags and provokes. She calls him dreadful, insulting, injuring things in public. She flays him with words. She says he's impotent: an artistic failure. I've heard her. Everyone has. When finally he lashes out, she's delighted. Her last husband beat hell out of her. She's a born victim.'

Alison takes Erica to a free solicitor, who – surprise, surprise – is efficient and who collects evidence and affidavits from doctors and hospitals all over London,

has a restraining order issued against Derek, gets Libby
and Erica back into the matrimonial home, and starts
and completes divorce proceedings and gets handsome
alimony. It all takes six months, at the end of which
time Erica's face has altogether lost its battered look.

Alison turns up at work the morning after the
alimony details are known and has the door shut in
her face. Mauromania. The lettering is flaking. The
door needs repainting.

Hugo sells the house over Alison's head. By this time
she and the children are living in a two-room flat.

Bad times.

'You're a very destructive person,' says Maureen to
Alison in the letter officially terminating her appointment. 'Derek never did you any harm, and you've
ruined his life, you've interfered in a marriage in a really
wicked way. You've encouraged Derek's wife to break
up his perfectly good marriage, and turned Derek's
child against him, and not content with that you've
crippled Derek financially. Erica would never have
been so vindictive if she hadn't had you egging her
on. It was you who made her go to law, and once
things get into lawyers' hands they escalate, as who
better than I should know? The law has nothing to do
with natural justice, idiot Alison. Hugo is very con-
cerned for you and thinks you should have mental
treatment. As for me, I am really upset. I expected
friendship and loyalty from you, Alison; I trained you
and employed you, and saw you through good times
and bad. I may say, too, that your notion of Mauromania becoming an exclusive fashion house, which I

followed through for a time, was all but disastrous, and symptomatic of your general bad judgment. After all, this is the people's age, the sixties, the seventies, the eighties, right through to the new century. Derek is coming in with me in the new world Mauromania.'

Mauromania, meretricious!

A month or so later, Derek and Maureen are married. It's a terrific wedding, somewhat marred by the death of Ruthie – killed, with her new baby, in the Paris air crash, on her way home from Istanbul, where she'd been trying to get her young husband released from prison. She'd failed. But then, if she'd succeeded, he'd have been killed too, and he was too young to die. Little Poppy was at the memorial service, in a sensible trousersuit from C & A, bought for her by Gran, without her glasses, both enormous eyes apparently now functioning well. She didn't remember Alison, who was standing next to her, crying softly. Soft beds of orange feathers, far away, another world.

Alison wasn't asked to the wedding, which in any way clashed with the mass funeral of the air-crash victims. Just as well. What would she have worn?

It's 1975.

It's summer, long and hot. Alison walks past Mauromania. Alison has remarried. She is happy. She didn't know that such ordinary everyday kindness could exist and endure. Alison is wearing, like everyone else, jeans and a T-shirt. A new ordinariness, a common sense, a serio-cheerfulness infuses the times. Female breasts swing free, libertarian by day, erotic by night, costing nobody anything, or at most a little modesty. No profit there.

Mauromania is derelict, boarded up. A barrow outside is piled with old stock, sale-priced. Coloured tights, fun-furs, feathers, slinky dresses. Passers-by pick over the stuff, occasionally buy, mostly look, and giggle, and mourn, and remember.

Alison, watching, sees Maureen coming down the steps. Maureen is rather nastily dressed in a bright yellow silk shift. Maureen's hair seems strange, bushy in parts, sparse in others. Maureen has abandoned her hat. Maureen bends over the barrow, and Alison can see the bald patches on her scalp.

'Alopecia,' says Alison, out loud. Maureen looks up. Maureen's face seems somehow worn and battered, and old and haunted beyond its years. Maureen stares at Alison, recognising, and Maureen's face takes on an expression of half-apology, half-entreaty. Maureen wants to speak.

But Alison only smiles brightly and lightly and walks on.

'I'm afraid poor Maureen has alopecia, on top of everything else,' she says to anyone who happens to enquire after that sad, forgotten figure, who once had everything – except, perhaps, a sense of sisterhood.

1976